To my readers

ALSO BY VERA BROOK

NOVELS

SAND RUNNER

GHOST RUNNER

SHORT FICTION

REX

THE OPPOSITE OF LUCK

HOW DREA GOT AN (ALMOST NEW) ARM

CAGE RUNNER

Book 2 in the Sand Runner Series

Vera Brook

Vera Brook

CAGE RUNNER

To learn more about Vera's writing and other creative endeavors, visit her website at www.verabrook.com, and follow her on Goodreads or Twitter.

Cover design by Vera Brook.

ISBN-13: 978-17327125-1-5

Second Paperback Edition: March 2020

CAGE RUNNER

1
KAI

THE ROBOTIC ARM swung at him out of nowhere, its four joints bending and rotating in a blind, preprogrammed motion. The welding tip, already white hot under the smashed sensor, aimed at his face.

At full speed, Kai veered to the right.

He dodged the arm a split second before the nozzle reached its phantom target—a car frame that wasn't there—and ignited a shower of sparks that would have burned his clothes and skin right off.

He exhaled and raced on, down a narrow path along a speeding conveyor belt, the frayed edges sharp like a chainsaw, less than ten feet of space separating him from the wire wall of the cage that enclosed the track and the runners on it.

"Go! Go! Go! Go!"

The audience's roar was like a second heartbeat pounding in his ears, wave after wave of it crashing into him from above, driving him forward.

Kai glanced up.

A stomping, fist-pumping crowd of men and women lined the observation deck that ran the length of the building. Tough and distrustful, they were residents of the lawless and rapidly disintegrating outer sectors of the megacity. By day, they hustled in the streets, their faces covered with masks to keep them from choking on the toxic city air. But by night, when the air was cooler and easier to breathe, the masks were off, and they all gathered here, to watch their favorite live entertainment.

The cage race was happening in an abandoned car manufacturing plant that sprawled three city blocks. In its heyday, a few decades ago, the place had been the poster image of technological development and economic prosperity. Rows upon rows of sleek machines had worked around the clock, with speed and precision no human worker could match, and a shiny new luxury car rolled off the assembly line every nine minutes.

3D printing put an end to it overnight. It produced no material waste and allowed infinite customization. And instead of a hundred specialized machines, the job could be done with one. When the plant closed its doors, the machines, suddenly obsolete, were left behind. Until someone came up with the idea of smashing the sensors and ripping out the safety locks, and using the robots as obstacles in an ultimate, winner-takes-all, adrenaline-pumping race.

"Go! Go! Go! Go!"

More robotic arms sprung up in Kai's path, sometimes several at once, as they cycled through their automatic routines, their welding tips, spraying nozzles, and grippers reaching for his flesh. When he couldn't get around them, he leapt and climbed over them, or dipped to his knees and slid underneath. But he dodged them all and kept running.

He was in the lead, but not by much. He risked a glance behind him.

Death Wish, a massive, one-eyed man, had just grabbed the two robotic nozzles that had pointed at him, and torn them right off their bases, one with each hand, before tossing them aside like two dead snakes.

The crowd howled in approval. They respected physical strength, and Death Wish was one of their favorites.

Ronny, who ran the place, spit on the floor, annoyed. Kai caught a warning look from him as he sprinted past. *Don't even think about it.* Death Wish was one of them, so he could get away with it. But Kai wouldn't.

Ronny preferred for the runners to damage each other and leave the machines be. Runners were easier to replace.

That was fine with Kai. He intended to win the race in the dullest possible way—by never giving his competitors a chance to catch up.

He also didn't give a damn about being part of the group. Most of the cage runners knew one another. But he preferred to stay a stranger, unrecognized and unbothered, minding his own business.

He was here for the cash reward and to get out of his own head. That was all. As soon as he crossed the finish line and collected the ancient but untraceable paper money, he'd be on his way.

His first few cage races nearly got him killed, the wire enclosure stirring some deep, primal anger at being trapped, and the screaming, taunting audience shattering his focus at every step.

But once he learned to shut them out, his training for the No Limits Race served him well. His reflexes were honed to perfection, and his endurance still top-notch, despite the harsh city air that burned like sand in his throat. And even though he'd blown his last service appointment with Neen, his prosthetic feet hadn't let him down yet.

Kai...

The voice was as real as if she stood next to him. Kai's hand shot to his ear, his fingertip touching the scar left behind by the communication link he'd used to talk to her during the Race.

But the com link wasn't there, and neither was his

Agent. Kai hadn't seen her for months, and he still had no idea where she was or why she'd left in the first place.

He dropped his hand and ran harder.

Up ahead, a stamping press the size of a house blocked the track, framed by two powerful grippers. The press was motionless like a rock, the heavy ram high in its shaft, leaving a wide opening to the other side.

Kai eyed the opening. Sliding through it would be the fastest way across.

"Go! Go! Go!" The audience spurred him on.

Suddenly, one gripper spun around and reached inside the opening, feeding it a non-existent sheet of metal. As soon as it withdrew, the press shuddered to life, and the ram dropped down, slamming into the die with enough force to bend a plate of steel. As the ram rose back into the shaft, another gripper went through the motions of picking up the phantom part and depositing it on the conveyor belt.

Another few seconds of stillness, and the routine started again.

Up close, the punch of the ram was like an explosion. It rattled Kai's bones.

Something dark in him urged him to do it, to hurl himself into the machine.

Kai, don't...

He clenched his fists, willing his mind to focus on the race, the race and nothing else.

But he didn't take the fast route under the ram. Instead, he leaned forward, gathering speed, and then half ran, half climbed up the face of the press, steering clear of the flywheel.

He got to the top and straightened, ready to cross it and jump off the other side—when he saw her.

She was here. On the crowded observation deck. Looking straight at him.

Emily.

Kai skidded to a stop, his heart racing and his mind spinning. Was it possible?

Then the crowd shifted, and she was gone.

"Em!" Kai sprang after her—and nearly walked off the edge.

He'd forgotten how high he was, the top of the press almost level with the observation deck twenty yards away. But how to get across? He cast a frantic look around him. Climbing down would be too slow, the gripper and the conveyor belt in the way. He glanced up.

A long, narrow steel beam ran overhead, connecting the far walls of the building, with lights and video cameras mounted underneath it. It would take him straight where he needed to go, if he could only reach it...

The flywheel! He could step on the frame.

He was already turning when the press shuddered underneath him, throwing him off balance.

So he was ill prepared for the attack—a vicious punch to the side of his ribs that brought him to his knees.

Death Wish had caught up with him, and he wanted blood.

For a moment, Kai was back in the No Limits Race and stunned that the other runner would engage in physical contact. Then pain hit him, his whole side on fire, and he remembered.

This was a cage race, and fights were part of the show. Someone like Death Wish didn't just outrun his opponents—he eliminated them.

The roar of the crowd became deafening. They'd seen Death Wish in action. They knew what was coming. And they were hungry.

"Fight! Fight! Fight! Fight!"

Kai pulled himself up and faced his opponent.

Death Wish grinned and cracked his knuckles, his

arm muscles bulging under thick scars. Half of his face was mangled by a nasty burn, but his good eye was fixed on Kai.

A normal reaction would be fear or anger. But instead, impatience surged through Kai like an electric current, burning in his gut. He didn't have time for this. The race no longer mattered. He found Emily, and he couldn't risk losing her again.

"Fight! Fight! Fight! Fight!"

Kai glanced behind him.

It was her! Her fingers gripping the wire fence and her eyes calling to him.

He barely had time to spin back before Death Wish advanced, his huge fist aimed at Kai's face.

It was now or never. Kai dodged the one-eyed man, leapt onto the flywheel, and propelled himself upward, his hands already reaching for the beam.

But he never made it. A hand gripped his arm and yanked him down, wrecking his trajectory and putting him into a half-spin.

For a moment he was airborne and disoriented, the press rushing upward and the gripper blurring past him, the sharp metal passing within an inch of his arm. Then gravity assist in his prostheses kicked into gear, pulling him into a vertical position, and he landed on the floor on the other side of the press.

Only it wasn't the floor.

The surface under his feet shifted like quicksand. He looked down, and terror gripped him. He was standing on top of the scrap metal disposal.

He tried to bolt—but it was too late.

The metal-crushing jaws split open, and Kai fell ankle deep into them. He made a desperate attempt to free himself, but the jaws were already closing, the teeth coming together with a sickening, grinding noise.

Above him, the crowd screamed, stomped, and

rocked the wire walls of the cage.

"Die! Die! Die! Die!"

But the sounds grew muffled and distant, his own heartbeat growing louder in his ears, counting down to the inevitable.

Kai...

He scanned the faces. Searching for her, needing to see her—then finding her.

Emily stared at him through the wire, her eyes wide with horror.

Except... it wasn't Emily.

The girl was a stranger.

Emily was never here. He never saw her, never heard her voice. It was all in his head.

But he was out of time.

Agony slammed into him, more intense than he'd ever known.

And then—darkness.

2
KAI

KAI WOKE UP flat on his back in a dim room that reeked of disinfectants, printing resin, and sweat.

Where was he?

His thoughts were sluggish, his body heavy and numb. With some effort, he turned his head and looked at the nearby wall. He squinted at the rows of objects on the shelves... and recoiled.

Even in the near darkness, he recognized the shape.

Legs. Cut off at the thigh and mounted upright. Some were human. Others looked like they once belonged to large birds, dogs, or horses. A few legs were intact, but on most of them, a patch of skin had been rolled up, exposing the muscles, tendons, and bones underneath.

Kai was wide awake now. Memories of the last cage race rushed at him—the robotic arms swinging at him, the punch of the press slamming into the die, the steel jaws biting into his prosthetic feet and pulling him under.

His feet!

He tried to sit up—but couldn't. A thick, padded restraint fit tightly across his chest and arms, holding him in place. No wonder he was stiff.

He lifted his chin to his chest, trying to see his legs. But a web of wires and tubes mounted on metal scaffolding blocked his view. He could feel the muscles in his abdomen tighten and strain. But below that—nothing.

No pain, no stiffness, no sensation whatsoever.

Terror crawled over his skin as he remembered the metal-crushing jaws closing around his robotic ankles, punching through the outer casing, wrecking the electronic circuits, ripping out his very nerves.

What happened to his legs? Did he still have them? He had already gone through this hell once, when he first came to the megacity. When he let them cut off his feet so he could be a Runner in the No Limits Race.

But he wasn't alone then. He had Emily. Even if he had no idea then how much she would mean to him—more than anybody or anything else, ever.

Now Emily was gone.

Eighty-seven days and counting.

The room spun around him, and Kai gripped the edges of the bed. He needed something to hold on to, something to keep him from falling, from tumbling down into an abyss that was rushing at him.

"Hey! Is anyone there?" His voice was hoarse. He struggled against the restraint. "What the hell is this?"

Only moments later voices and hurried footsteps came from behind the door.

"Why is he awake?"

"I couldn't risk a higher dose. He lost a lot of blood."

"I need more time. Talk to him. Just not about—"

"I know, I know."

The door opened, and harsh lights filled the room. Two people rushed toward Kai.

He blinked at them, his eyes burning from the brightness.

It was Andy and Neen. His former Technician and Print Maker.

"What is this? Get this thing off me." He made another effort to free himself from the belt.

Andy's strong hands dropped onto Kai's shoulders,

pinning him to the bed. "If you want to walk again—*don't* move. Do you understand me?"

Relief surged through Kai. So walking wasn't out of the question. He needed to get the hell out of here.

"Okay." He shrugged off the Technician's hands.

They hadn't exactly been on friendly terms since Emily's disappearance. Andy had never been talkative. But now Kai suspected he knew more than he was letting on, and that was enough to put him on edge.

Neen hurried to the foot of the bed. "You shouldn't be awake yet," she grumbled.

Kai relaxed a little. He still couldn't feel anything. No sensory feedback from the prostheses at all. But Neen was working on it. And if anyone could fix him up, it was her.

Although Neen wasn't much older than Kai, who was seventeen, she had already made a name for herself as one of the best prosthetics experts in the Alliance. Kai was a living proof of that. Neen had designed and printed all the prostheses he had worn in the Race, and he made it through each grueling course alive and mostly unharmed.

His only complaint, then and now, was that she seemed to care more about the stunning bionic feet she created than about the Runner they were attached to. But maybe that wasn't fair of him. Neen wasn't like anyone else he knew. 3D printing was her calling, her passion, her sole purpose in life. She didn't seem to need anyone or anything else.

Sometimes Kai envied her.

He glanced at the shelves again. In the bright light, the legs looked less menacing. They were probably synthetic replicas, maybe even functional prostheses. But maybe not. It was hard to tell with Neen. A cut wire or fried circuit upset her more than blood pouring from a flesh wound.

"What the hell were you thinking, Kai?" Andy's voice yanked him back.

Kai kept his gaze on the shelf, pretending to study the intricate arrangement of muscles in one specimen. This was not a conversation he wanted to have. "I need the money."

"Bullshit. You have a job."

"Yeah. A test monkey."

"So you prefer to get killed?"

Kai's mind swung back to the cage race. To the urge to dive under the bone-shattering punch of the press, the fastest way across. To Death Wish's murderous, one-eyed glare. To the crowd screaming, *Die! Die! Die! Die!* To the metal teeth crushing his prosthetic feet and ripping them from his flesh.

He shook off the memory. "What do you want from me? I'm a Runner, remember? This is what I trained for."

No. It's what *Emily* trained him for.

He saw her as clearly as if she was in front of him, and the familiar hollow pain filled him.

"Why don't you go home?" Andy said.

Kai shot him a look. "Yeah, right."

Andy knew damn well Kai couldn't leave. Not until he found her. Not until she looked him in the eye and told him the truth, told him what happened.

Andy kept trying to convince him to let it go. If Emily left, she must have had a good reason. Kai was wasting his time trying to find her.

But Kai wasn't buying it. He'd been searching for her, on and off, for three months. Something must have happened, or she wouldn't have left the way she did—without any warning whatsoever, when he was sleeping. He had to see her and make sure she was okay.

"Wait. How did you and Neen find me?" he asked.

Andy's lips were a thin line of disapproval. "Dumb

luck. Someone posted a message online."

Wild hope flared in Kai's chest. "*Who?*"

"It was anonymous."

"What did it—*ARGH!*" Kai's words turned into a garbled scream as a million burning pins cut into his flesh. He strained against the belt, his vision blurring.

"I got it. I got it." Neen was working hurriedly, her head bent low. "How's that? Better?"

The pain abruptly stopped, leaving only a tingling sensation. Kai let out a sharp breath. "Yeah. Thanks."

Neen pulled away the scaffolding. She was done.

Andy leaned forward and unfastened the restraint. "Okay, mate. Easy does it."

But Kai was already sitting up and swinging his legs over the edge of the bed. He flexed each foot, drew a circle in the air. They felt fine. Even better than the prostheses he wrecked in the cage race. Neen never stopped improving her designs.

He stood up and took a step.

It was like the shelf rushed toward him, and he nearly slammed into it. Instead of advancing a single step, his new feet had whisked him a good three yards.

"I'm fine." Kai waved it off. "I've got it."

The problem wasn't the prostheses anyway. He was just distracted.

Someone who knew him had been at the cage race, watching him, and that someone had called for help. It was a long shot, but Kai didn't care. A long shot was better than nothing.

"Where the hell are you going?" Andy yelled.

But Kai was already out the door.

3
EMILY

EMILY STOOD in front of a large hologram, her eyes and hands moving urgently over the display. The hologram mimicked a computer screen but hovered a foot away from a gray wall, adding to the illusion of space. Two more walls enclosed the small cubicle, which was empty except for a tall narrow desk holding a docking station. A flexible tablet stuck out of it, producing the projection.

"Oh, come on," Emily muttered, as her fingers narrowly missed a cube-shaped folder. It hurled away from her, spinning. A moment later, it shrunk to a dot and was gone.

Beyond her cubicle were rows of other cubicles, all of them empty. The building, once teeming with office workers, was now abandoned. Dim light seeped in through tall windows, the glass coated with twenty years of smog and grime.

The database Emily was working on was unlike anything she'd ever seen. Whole sections of it shifted and morphed every few seconds, causing all search algorithms to fail. Maybe if the database was smaller, that wouldn't be an issue. But it held huge amounts of data, organized into several dozen of levels and crosslinked in strange ways. Add the relentless motion, which made the whole structure look different from one moment to the next, and the task became infuriating enough that any other hacker would throw up her hands in frustration and walk away.

But walking away was a luxury Emily didn't have.

Not now, not ever. She had been through too much to get this far, and she had put others through even more. After all, the only reason she'd become an Agent was to get close to this database, even if the work kept her too busy to make much progress until the Race was over.

Her fingers nearly grasped another folder, shaped like a cone. But the database morphed again, the folder stretching and thinning until it was a flat tile. The tile sped across the display, slicing through a dense block of folders that shattered like glass.

Emily reflexively pulled her hands back. "No way!"

She had spent the last three months trying every trick she could think of, with no success. She was determined to keep at it until she cracked the database open and found what she needed in there. But some days, after hours of staring at the shifting shapes that seemed to mock her, dark doubts gripped her.

What if she failed? What would happen then?

And even if she succeeded, would it make a difference—or was she only deluding herself?

A footstep sounded behind her.

Emily spun around.

But there was no one there.

It was strange. Plenty of good fortune had come her way, more than she deserved, and much of it owed to one person. But all that good luck only made her more wary, more distrustful. She knew it wouldn't hold. And this time, if she made a mistake, it would be over.

Better not to dwell on it, though. She turned her attention back to the screen.

The database was like some alien hive reacting with alarm to an intruder, sections of it sliding and stretching in different directions, merging and dividing, swapping places, rushing to the surface or dropping out of sight.

She suspected the patterns were preset, and the system cycled through them, whether anyone was looking or not, but she couldn't be sure. If it just didn't cycle through them so damn fast.

"I need you to be still," Emily spoke to the screen. "Can you do that for me? I'm asking you nicely."

At least the access wasn't an issue. She had managed to create a phantom, low-level admin account when she resided in the Training Center and could hack the security system from within. Now she used it to slip past the firewall and into the database more or less undetected. Of course, as she quickly discovered, entering the database was no guarantee that she could open and read the files. But it brought her a step closer.

It was all there, all the evidence she would ever need, updated in real time. If she could only get to it.

A window popped open in the corner of her screen. It was an alert she'd set up.

She made a swiping motion with her hand, and the live news story filled the display. Another swipe, and the cubicle filled with voices and shuffling feet.

"Mr. Hollenbach! Mr. Hollenbach!"

Instantly tense, Emily stepped back to watch.

On the screen, a press conference was in progress, the room packed with reporters, all pushing and raising their hands to ask a question.

Emily stared in disbelief at the two men behind the podium. The older man, regal and white-haired, fielded the reporters' questions. The younger one, with cold, cruel eyes, stood silently a few feet behind him.

Slayer and his father. Or Marcus Hollenbach and his son and heir, Julian Hollenbach. Two of the wealthiest men in the megacity. Apparently reconciled.

"No way," she whispered.

Maybe a different man could forgive his father for sentencing him to the most brutal race on the planet. But not Slayer. Slayer never forgave. She knew that with the same certainty she knew that one day he would track her down, and she would pay for making him lose the Race.

"Last question, folks!" A voice called out.

A female reporter with a sharp, triangular face spoke up. "A merger between BioPrintex and 3D Electronics would let you control the entire health technology market. Why did you call it off? Any chance you'll reconsider?"

"*No.* My decision is final." Hollenbach's voice rang with authority. He didn't elaborate.

Emily's gaze moved to Slayer.

His face gave nothing away. But he knew why the merger was off, even if the press and the public didn't. And so did she.

It had to do with last year's No Limits Race. The Race had been rigged, a secret deal struck between BioPrintex and 3D Electronics to ensure that the top two spots went to their own Runners. Slayer was supposed to win, Kai to finish a close second. What better way to promote the future merger of the two corporations than a nearly shared victory of their Runners in the most popular and widely watched competition on the planet?

Except Kai would have none of it.

He threw his own chances to stop Slayer from grabbing the title he neither earned nor deserved. Instead, Venus won, and her victory changed everything. What was meant to be a cunning advertising campaign turned into a wave of angry protests that spread around the globe like wildfire, and the merger was promptly called off.

Emily had to remind herself that the Runners' identities were hidden, their faces digitally altered in all video broadcasts. The reporters didn't know Julian

Hollenbach was really Slayer, any more than they knew the old Hollenbach forced his own son to compete in the Race to punish him for misusing the company's money. Slayer's official story on the show—a wealthy businessman bored with his posh lifestyle and craving excitement—was a lie. But it fit well enough to be believable.

Hollenbach's decision to back out of the merger must have been a serious setback for Falcon. *Good.*

The thought gave her a pause. Did it mean she and the head of BioPrintex were on the same side? What if she told him of her suspicions and asked for his help? He could be a powerful ally.

But she dismissed the idea. Why would Hollenbach care? Even if he and Falcon had publically broken off all their business dealings and, as a rumor had it, were no longer on speaking terms. Even if Falcon blamed Hollenbach for calling off the merger and thwarting his plans, and he moved to retaliate. The head of BioPrintex hardly needed Emily's help to deal with it.

So why would he help *her?*

Just then—Marcus Hollenbach shuddered and cried out, his hands clutching his chest.

Emily stared in shock.

It looked like the old Hollenbach was having a heart attack.

Slayer rushed forward. "Father?"

The old man stumbled, his eyes bulging and face contorting with agony. His son caught him before he collapsed. "We need a medic! Get me a medic! Now!"

Havoc broke out in the crowded room. People yelled and pushed each other for a better view. The sheer magnitude of the event was enough to rattle even the most seasoned reporters.

Emily couldn't believe her eyes.

The old Hollenbach had always been a paragon of health—his daily runs, swims, and sparing matches the subject of much publicity—adding to his already larger-than-life status as the head of one of the most powerful corporations in the world.

The heart attack was no natural occurrence.

Falcon was behind it.

She was sure of it.

Within seconds, a team of medics arrived. The unconscious magnate was hooked up to life support, lifted onto a stretcher, and rushed out the back door. Slayer never left his father's side.

Emily was still staring at the screen, trying to make sense of what happened, when the news segment ended and another began. The conference room disappeared, replaced by a large industrial vat with a glass insert. Inside the vat, a mass of winged insects teemed and crawled over one another.

Emily made a cutting motion with her hand, and the screen vanished, revealing a blank wall behind it. She lifted the tablet from the docking station, slipped it inside her backpack, and strapped the pack on.

She had stayed in this building for almost a week. It was time to move.

She had always known that Falcon would stop at nothing to carry out his plans. Under the guise of cool scientific intellect, the man was a ruthless fanatic. But it was still a shock to see this fanaticism in action. If he was willing to murder a business partner for bailing out on him, what would he do to her if he knew what she was planning?

She really didn't want to find out.

She turned and headed for the staircase.

When she got to the ground level, she pulled out a face mask and slipped it on over her mouth and nose. She unzipped the collar of her jacket and pulled out a large, segmented hood that covered her head and the top half of her face. She adjusted the mesh visor until it was over her eyes and she could see through it.

Then she pushed out the door and into the street.

4
KAI

EVEN RUNNING at a good clip, it took Kai three hours to get to the manufacturing plant that housed the last cage race. Taking a hover cab would've been faster, but he was short on cash and preferred to travel on foot anyway.

He knew the general direction ahead of time but picked his route on a hunch, scanning each street and alley he ran on, searching for the familiar silhouette.

It was a habit by now. He was always searching for her.

There were still whole sectors of the megacity Kai had never seen, including some in the business district with no passable streets at all, the massive buildings so close together they seemed to grow on top of each other and so tall their roofs vanished in the smog.

But the outer sectors were more familiar by now. Particularly the vast, industrial sector that stretched from the border of the business district all the way to the west horizon and housed a dozen ghetto neighborhoods that by all economic metrics should have died out decades ago. But they were still hanging on, still surviving, although Kai had no idea how.

Most people he passed on the streets wore face masks or deep hoods that hid their eyes. Some wore jackets with human faces painted on the sleeves and back. Kai had been puzzled by the strange fashion until he realized it was purely practical. People around here guarded their identity closely. The fake faces were popular because they confused the facial recognition software used by the drones.

The drones were a constant presence, some hovering in place, others flying along the streets. There were so many of them that he eventually stopped noticing them at all.

He should be wearing a mask or a hood too. His exposed head and face only attracted attention. More than once, a drone followed him for several blocks or dropped down in front of him with the camera pointed straight at his face, so close he could see his own reflection in the lens.

He always stopped and stared back when that happened, full of anticipation.

Emily had used a drone to find him and talk to him, back when she first recruited him to be a Runner. Maybe she was using a drone again, for whatever purpose.

If she did, he wanted her to see him.

The manufacturing plant looked even more decrepit in daylight, the paint faded and peeling off the cracked wall like old skin, the windows boarded up where the glass had been smashed, and plastic trash lining the curbs and lodged in every crevice. All of it covered with city dust that hadn't seen rain for months.

Inside, on the main floor, Ronny worked on one of the robots. He dropped the screwdriver when Kai walked in. "I'll be damned. I saw the shredder rip off your feet. But look at you now. Good as new." He stared at Kai's prostheses, the design a tad too sleek to pass for a normal shoe. Then he looked Kai in the eye. "So you're a Runner, eh? The Sponsor will always fix you up?"

Kai tensed. Prostheses weren't against the rules. Plenty of cage runners had mechanical arms or legs. And he wasn't going to discuss Peter Falcon with Ronny.

"Something like that. Listen, I need to ask you something."

Ronny flashed his crooked teeth. To him, every favor was a transaction, to be repaid at a later time and with interest. "What do you need, Runner?"

"I'm... looking for someone." Kai's throat tightened. Why was this so hard? "There was a girl on the deck. I think she saved my life."

"Girl? What girl?" Ronny frowned. "*I* saved your life."

"You posted the message?"

"No. I hit the shutdown button!" Ronny was getting all worked up. Kai was far from showing proper gratitude. "And I've got to tell you, the race was a dud after that. The damn robots wouldn't restart. The fans tore down part of the wire, they were so mad. See over there?" He pointed. "It's going to cost me an arm and a leg to fix."

"I'm sorry for your trouble," Kai said. "And I appreciate what you did. But someone posted a message to alert my..." He hesitated over how to describe Andy and Neen. "Friends. And I think it was that girl."

Ronny bent down and grabbed the screwdriver off the floor. "You think I have time to watch everyone who comes in here? As long as they pay the ticket and don't bring the place down, I don't care what they do." He started tightening a screw on the robotic arm. "I'm running a business here. I have other things to worry about."

"You have security cameras," Kai pressed on. "If I could watch the footage..."

Ronny's face turned a blotchy red. "You want to watch the footage from security cameras? And what, maybe make a copy and take it to some fancy lawyer? That the plan?" He aimed the screwdriver at Kai like a knife. "Get out of here, Runner. I don't need any trouble from you."

"Forget it." Kai said, his only hope, his only lead, crumbling to dust. "I was done here, anyway."

He looked up at the empty observation deck as he headed for the door. Was it Emily he'd seen there during the race? Did she follow him somehow, come to watch him, but didn't want him to know, didn't want him to see her? But why not? And where was she now? The question had been eating at him for three months.

He stepped outside and started walking faster and faster, until he was running, blind with anger.

He passed a building gutted by fire, then another half-collapsed in the middle, as if a giant fist smashed through it. Soon, nothing looked familiar. But Kai didn't care where he went, as long as he was moving. Except it still wasn't fast enough, so he pumped harder, until he was nearly flying down the empty streets, past one abandoned building after another, his prosthetic feet barely touching the dusty ground.

Emily.

He had to find her. He didn't care how far he had to go or how long it took. He wasn't going to stop until he did.

When his eyes started to sting, he blinked and rubbed at them with the heels of his hands, furious with himself. Hell no. He was *not* going to cry. He gritted his teeth and raced on.

But his eyes kept stinging, and it got worse. Now his nose and mouth were burning too, then his throat. It was the air. Sharp and cutting. Chemical. Hard to breath... and getting harder.

It made Kai think of a sand storm. Except there was no sand. Whatever was in the air was too small to see.

He slowed to a walk. It was impossible to run. His legs were heavy. He inhaled hungrily, but the burning air only made him weaker. He couldn't get enough oxygen into his lungs.

Then he sensed something and turned behind him.

A block or so away, a stone wall had risen between the buildings.

Kai stared at it in confusion. Where did it come from? He'd just walked through there.

Then the wall pressed closer, no longer solid but shifting and swirling like a thick cloud.

Smog.

"Red sands," Kai muttered.

The mass of noxious smoke advanced toward him. It seemed almost alive. A faceless monster reaching for him with a hundred arms, then surging ahead and engulfing him.

The next breath he took was like swallowing fire, the poisonous air scorching his nose and throat, squeezing tears from his eyes. He started coughing, but that only made it worse. His vision blurred, and he stumbled, the pressure in his lungs building, becoming unbearable. He couldn't breathe. It was like drowning without water.

Kai, keep going. You have to keep going.

Stopping was a mistake. He should have run. Now the smog was all around him, so thick he couldn't see his own feet. He took a step and tripped on something. He turned and walked into a wall.

Goddamnit. He didn't want to die. He had to find Emily.

He was half-blind and barely standing, with one hand on the wall for support, when a door swung open and hands grabbed him and spun him around.

Kai caught a glimpse of a terrifying gas mask on his attacker's face.

And then he was roughly pulled inside.

5
KAI

INSIDE THE HOUSE, Kai threw a blind punch in a desperate attempt at self-defense. But his lungs were bursting and his vision nearly gone, and he missed. Already off balance, a shove to the back sent him sprawling across the hard floor.

The door slammed shut, and several blurry shapes drew closer. He made out heavy boots. Several pairs of them.

It was over. He was trapped and outnumbered. He was going to die here.

The masked boy stepped around Kai and swung a kick at a large drum. The thing shook, and long blades started turning inside it, hissing madly.

An electric fan.

Cool air hit Kai's face, and he gulped it down greedily, the pain in his chest easing and his vision returning. He glanced around him and counted at least ten people. Too many to fight. Escape was his only chance.

"What the hell is this?" An angry voice came from the far end of the room. The man had a stocky build and blazing red hair. He walked with a limp, but it didn't slow him down, and he was heading straight for Kai. The others stepped aside to let him pass.

Kai pushed to his feet, ready to face him. His gaze snapped to the door. A few more breaths, and he could make a run for it.

But the red-haired man crossed to the fan and kicked the switch. The blades slowed, and the air stopped blowing. "You went outside in this weather?" He glared at the boy wearing the gas mask. "Are you out of your mind?"

The boy yanked the mask off his face—and it wasn't a boy at all. It was a girl! And judging by her flaming hair, she and the man were siblings.

"What was I supposed to do? Watch him die out there?" The girl argued, not intimidated in the least. "He didn't even have a mask!"

Her brother's face was hard. "That's his problem. Not yours."

"How can you say that? Look at this!" She pointed out the window, where the toxic clouds raged past like torrents of dirty water, blotting out all daylight. "A few more minutes and he would've been dead!" She tossed her short red hair angrily. "Is that what you want us to be? So cold and heartless we'd watch someone die and not lift a finger to help them?"

Kai watched her in amazement.

She had saved his life, and now she was defending him. Why? She didn't even know him.

The brother took a step toward the girl, raising his arm. "You—"

Without thinking, Kai jumped between them and caught his wrist. "Don't do that."

The man blinked in surprise. Then he yanked his wrist free and snatched the girl's gas mask. "*You're* staying inside. Understood?"

The girl ignored him, her attention entirely on Kai. "Don't worry. Val would never hit me. But that was brave of you."

Kai held her gaze. She had pretty, gray eyes, and her skin was so pale, it looked almost translucent.

"You saved my life," he said simply.

The girl blushed.

A low growl issued from Val's throat. "Okay, pal. I've had enough of you."

Kai braced himself for a fight, but a young boy wearing thick glasses elbowed his way closer. He pointed at Kai's prosthetic feet. "Whoa! Guys—look at the gear!"

Kai froze, every muscle in his body tense.

There was a reason why Runners' identities were protected. How many of the people staring him down had lost money betting on him in the Race? Those who had probably weren't happy he threw away his shot at victory to help another Runner. How long before they realized who he was? He needed to get out of here.

A grimace twisted Val's face, his gaze sliding down to Kai's feet. "Upgraded, eh? You got money to burn?"

Icy sweat slicked Kai's back. People never expected to cross paths with a Runner in real life. Maybe he could still keep his cover. "I wish. It was for a job. I was a... test monkey." It wasn't far from the truth.

Val's eyes narrowed. "And they let you keep them?"

Kai shrugged. "For now. They don't know I quit yet." He glanced at the faces around him, hoping for a laugh, but no such luck.

They just watched him.

Only the boy with glasses was clearly pumped. "Guys! This is so cool! He can *help* us!"

"We don't need any help." Val's tone was sharp, his expression stone cold. He looked Kai straight in the eye. "So you better get on your way."

But the girl stepped forward and touched her brother's arm. "Val, come on. He can't go anywhere right now. How about we discuss it tomorrow?"

*

It was night by the time the smog let up, leaving as abruptly as it had arrived. Kai was awake, stretched on a thin mattress and gazing out the window when the street outside turned pitch black.

He had an impulse to get up and leave. He'd counted eleven people earlier—seven men and four women, all close to his age—and they all slept elsewhere in the house. No one would notice if he stepped out the door. And even if they did, they'd never catch him if he took off running.

But something stopped him.

For one, he knew he was in no immediate danger. Even if most of the group wasn't particularly welcoming, and Val, the leader, openly disliked him, once it was decided Kai would stay the night, no one as much as spoke a harsh word to him. They simply accepted it and went about their business. And the girl, Leah, was genuinely friendly and made sure he got something to eat and a mattress to sleep on, before she bid him a timid goodnight and withdrew to the back of the house.

But there was more. Kai was curious about the group, curious about how they lived, how they survived. He kept thinking about what the boy with thick glasses, whom everyone called Green, had said. Could Kai really help them? *How?* The idea excited him and filled him with sadness at the same time. It had been a while since anyone needed his help.

Once the idea took hold of him, he couldn't get rid of it. He tossed and turned on his makeshift bed, exhausted but unable to sleep, hoping that a group of strangers would trust him enough to give him a job. Anything. He wasn't picky.

And who knew, maybe they had some information he could use, something that would put him on the right track and help him in his search.

*

Dawn was breaking when Kai heard the familiar limping gait. Val was up and heading for the door, without a single glance in Kai's direction. He carried a large backpack.

A few others walked behind him, with similar backpacks and the same determined expressions on their faces. Their eyes slid over the lone visitor but didn't linger. Only Green nodded to Kai in passing.

That scrap of encouragement did it. Kai jumped to his feet and cleared his throat. "Hey."

Val paused and turned to him. "You're still here." He wasn't going to make it easy.

"I..." Kai racked his mind for the right word. *Help* was out of the question. "I owe you." He scanned the faces but didn't find Leah. "*All* of you."

It was true. Leah saved his life, so his biggest debt was to her. But he owed all of them, including Val. They could've turned him out, but they hadn't.

"Is that right?" Val's tone was still cold, but his shoulders relaxed. He stuck his thumbs under the straps of his backpack and waited.

"Yeah." Kai tried to sound casual. "You mind if I tag along?"

If Val said *no*, he'd have no choice but to leave.

Just then, Leah trotted over. She was slightly out of breath and still zipping up her jacket, her red hair mussed from sleep.

Val's face changed when he saw her. "Where are *you* going?"

Leah threw him a sharp look. "Where do you think? I'm coming with you. You forgot to wake me." She pushed her messy hair out of her face and glanced at Kai, then quickly away.

"No, you're not. It's too—" Val started.

But Leah had turned on her heel and was already marching out the door.

"Fine." Val clenched his jaw and headed after her.

The others followed.

And since no one stopped him, so did Kai.

6
KAI

OUTSIDE, THE GROUP headed down the street, with Val setting a brisk pace.

Kai looked around as he walked, trying to place his current location on his mental map of the city. But he could see no landmarks he recognized, and the tall, narrow houses lining the street looked unfamiliar. They were also very old. Pressed wall to wall, they looked like they kept each other from collapsing. The stone walls crumbled with age, and debris blocked the sidewalks. In the middle of the street, deep cracks split the asphalt.

Kai tripped a few times before his new prostheses learned to navigate the terrain.

In between the swinging arms up ahead, he could see Val. His limp was more pronounced here, something wrong with his right knee. But he held his head high and never faltered, as if the uneven ground didn't bother him.

Kai respected that.

They walked for several more blocks, turning left, then right, then left again. No one spoke, whether on his account or not, Kai couldn't tell.

In the silence, his thoughts drifted to Emily and to the question that was never far from his thoughts.

Why had she left that day?

She and Kai had arrived in the city a few days earlier and had been staying with Neen and Andy. Emily had gotten stronger after the surgery and no longer used a cane when she walked. That alone made his heart sing for joy. If she grew quiet and distant sometimes, if she was still holding back, that was fine by him. He knew she cared about him, and that was all that mattered.

He didn't want to rush her. The Race was over, and they had all the time in the world.

So when he found her handwritten note that morning, his whole reality came crashing down like a sheet of glass.

"I have to leave. I can't explain. I'm sorry."

Leave to go where... and do what? And why couldn't she explain? What stopped her? Didn't she know she could trust him?

"I'm sorry."

No. He didn't believe it. There was more—there had to be. He had to find her and find out.

Kai...

If he focused, he could see her face in front of him.

"Kai."

He blinked, like waking from a dream. Gray eyes peered at him, and a slender hand brushed his arm. Leah.

"What?"

"We're going this way." She pointed behind her, where the group was filing into a dark, narrow alley between two buildings.

"Thanks." If she hadn't stopped him, he would've kept walking, his legs moving and his eyes scanning the ground, but his mind elsewhere, lost in a daydream. It wasn't the first time it happened. He'd been spending too much time on his own.

Val let the others pass to wait for his sister. "Leah. Come on." He threw a dark look in Kai's direction. *Stay away from her.*

Kai hid a smile. Val had him all wrong. The protective-brother act was touching but unnecessary.

The alley continued for several blocks, so narrow

that if he spread his arms, he could touch both walls.

The ground was littered with crumpled trash and occasionally blocked by piles of bricks or discarded furniture that had fallen from above. Kai kept glancing up at the bright strip of sky overhead, half expecting something to smash his skull at any point. There was no place to hide if that happened. All the doors they passed were bolted from the inside, and the windows were rare and high up, the lowest one on the third floor. The sooner they got out of the alley, the better.

But instead of open space, the alley spit them out under an old overpass. Resting on massive stone columns reinforced with steel, it rose fifty feet in the air like a wide river of cement seen from below, blocking most of the sky. Once, a roar of heavy traffic had to continually echo down from it, making the ground vibrate. But the overpass was dead silent now, not a single vehicle passing overhead.

A memory stirred in Kai's mind. The last, fateful obstacle course of the Race. He and three other Runners raced on an abandoned highway, leaping over barriers and dodging speeding cars. Venus, the only female Runner, took first place. But Kai scored a bigger victory, even if it was left out of the official broadcast—a one-on-one against Slayer, that cheating bastard. It still put a grin on Kai's face.

Val and the others continued on, deeper into the shadows of the overpass, and Kai followed.

It wasn't long before a shaft of light appeared ahead, illuminating the wreckage.

A long segment of the overpass had collapsed, taking with it dozens of cars and trucks that now lay piled up underneath it, a mass of jagged glass and warped metal. Above, huge slabs of cement still hung on steel rods, touching the top of the pile. More cars were visible on the surface, some distance away from the edge.

No wonder the overpass was quiet. Until the rupture was repaired, there was nowhere to go.

Kai caught up to the group, and they all surveyed the wreckage in awed silence. Kai glanced at Leah. She was pale as a ghost, her eyes wide in shock.

"Okay, listen up." Val turned to the others, and they shifted to face him in a half-circle. "It happened a week ago, so if you see someone inside the car, they're dead and you can't help them." He looked from one person to another. "But the pile could shift, so watch your back. Start with the cars at the edges." He gave his sister a pointed look. "You team with Ana, and... take it easy."

Ana was a tall brunette with piercing, dark eyes and a long, thick braid. She nodded to Val, and she and Leah headed off toward a truck sprawled across the ground some distance away from the main pile, the cargo container thrown on its side but the cabin still upright. The rest of the group dispersed as well.

"You ever scrapped before?" A voice asked, and Kai turned to see Green next to him.

"*Scrapped?*"

"You know—recycle, reuse, resell?" Green pulled off his glasses and wiped the thick lenses with his sleeve. "We do mostly electronics. But hey, if I find a pile of cash, I'll take that too." Green replaced his glasses on his nose and flashed a smile.

Kai smiled back. "Got it." It all suddenly made sense: the location, the backpacks. They were scavengers. "So what's good to scrap here?"

Green's eyes lit up. "Are you kidding? Lots of stuff." He scanned the cars nearby, deciding. Then picked one—a delivery van—and started walking. "Come on. I'll show you."

The van was scratched up, tires blown, windshields and headlights shattered, and the cargo compartment smashed in on one side. But considering how it got there, it didn't look bad.

Green nervously peered inside the cabin. "Empty," he reported, visibly relieved.

He pulled on the handle, and the door easily opened. He slipped in the driver's seat. Kai went around and got in on the passenger side.

"Okay. Watch this." Green shrugged off his backpack and rummaged inside for a screwdriver. Then, armed with this simple tool, he removed the casing around the steering wheel and proceeded to dismantle the cockpit computer. The GPS and the stereo were the first to go into the backpack. Then, one by one, several other electronic components and circuit boards were freed and slipped inside the pack as well.

Other tools briefly flashed in Green's hands to pry open lids or snip wires, and Kai thought of his friend Ron. Some people were offended that Ron fixed things instead of buying new, but that never bothered the old man. Scrapping sounded like something Ron would approve of, even if, technically, they were stealing.

"Let's check out the back." Green flipped a switch that unlocked the back door.

But when they got there, and Green pulled on the handle, the door was jammed. Unfazed, he produced another tool and pressed it to the door handle. There was a pop, and the door swung open.

"Air hammer. Very handy." Green put the tool away and faced the cargo in the van. "Holy smokes! Look at all that loot!" He left the backpack on the ground and leapt inside.

It turned out the van carried a large vending machine, which busted open when it fell off the overpass and slammed into the ground. Now twenty kinds of snacks in brightly-colored wrappers covered the floor.

Green whipped out a large bag and started loading it up, grinning from ear to ear. "Sweet, sweet, sweet."

Kai reached inside the van for a pack of peanuts and turned it in his fingers. "Real food?"

"You bet!" Green was still laughing, scooping the candy into the bag by the handful.

A sharp screech of metal made Kai look back over his shoulder, his gaze drawn to the pile of wreckage in the light.

A lonely figure was awkwardly climbing to the top, the layers of steel shifting and murmuring like sand under his feet.

One glance—and Kai dropped the snack and took off at a sprint.

He was halfway up the pile himself when the hair-raising sound of metal grinding and sliding against metal pierced the air, followed by a breathless cry, "*Val!*"

7
KAI

KAI HAD CLIMBED vertical cliffs before and leapt over chasms a hundred feet deep. But both paled in comparison to what he was doing right now—racing up a shifting mass of warped metal and shattered glass the size of a building, that threatened to topple down and swallow him at any moment.

Every shard of glass wanted to stab him. Every metal edge tried to slice him open. He quickly learned to use his bare hands as little as possible and instead relied on his prosthetic feet, which were sturdy enough to withstand the assault. One false step, one missed handhold, and it would be like falling into the shredder all over again, and not just his feet this time.

Kai had no plan for what to do when he caught up with Val. He acted on impulse. Val was in trouble, and that was enough to get Kai moving.

Now, up close, he saw that the red-haired man was stuck on a narrow ledge. A flattened sedan blocked his path, having rotated nearly ninety degrees after some pressure point had been removed by the disturbance. The driver's body was still inside.

Val reached in through the smashed windshield. A tool flashed in his hand.

Kai stared at him in disbelief. Did he climb up here just to find the body? And what was the tool for? Whatever it was, Val was nuts to take the risk. The sedan was motionless, but a grinding sound of crushed glass warned that some movement was occurring, and things could change at any moment.

"Watch out!" Kai called.

Val yanked his hand back and spun around, quickly pocketing the tool. He glared at Kai. "What the hell are you doing up here? Get back down."

Kai shook his head and pointed to the torn edge of the overpass above. "Too late. This whole pile is about to collapse. We've got to climb *up*." He tested his step and climbed on top of a bent hood, then onto the roof, to demonstrate.

Val looked up at the slab of cement hanging over the wreckage, twisted rods sticking out of it in all directions, and he scowled. "*You* go ahead." He took a stiff, shuffling step along the ledge, spotted a foothold below, and tried to step down.

He nearly fell off as the metal bumper broke off under his weight and tumbled down the pile. The sedan shuddered, glass crunching and metal grinding against metal.

Kai scanned the tangled mass of metal ahead. They were so close! They could make it. He stuck out his hand to Val. "Don't be stupid. Come on!"

"Forget it."

The grinding noise rose in pitch. The sedan was definitely moving, slipping out of the pile, dipping lower as gravity exerted its pull. And if it fell, it would take several more cars with it.

Kai was out of patience. "Climb, goddammit—or your sister will watch you die!"

Val glanced down at the ground, and the blood drained from his face.

Leah stared up at them, both hands clasped over her mouth. Ana moved closer and put an arm around her.

Val ignored Kai's hand, but he clambered on top of

the car roof. They started climbing side by side. And it was just in time. The whole pile seemed to come to life below them, shaking and rumbling menacingly.

"*Go! Go! Go!*" Kai yelled. He matched his speed to Val's, ready to jump to his aid.

But the red-haired man held his own. He was surprisingly fast. Growls of pain or frustration escaped his throat as he charged up the pile, battling with his stiff knee. But he kept moving.

They got to the top and started scaling the rods to the surface not a moment too soon.

The sedan came loose and fell twenty feet, smashing into a large trailer.

Several other wrecks followed, starting an avalanche of metal and glass, followed by a thick, billowing cloud of dust.

Val let go of the rod, as if to jump down. "Leah, get back!"

"Don't stop!" Kai urged. "Keep moving! Keep moving!" There was no guarantee that the slab of cement they were climbing wouldn't tumble down as well.

They reached the surface of the overpass and hoisted themselves over the edge. The sharp stone cut into Kai's palms and bruised his ribs, but they made it. They crawled away from the abyss, panting and coughing. Then they scrambled to their feet.

Val yanked a face mask from his pocket and put it on, pulled his hood over his head. He threw another mask to Kai. "Put this on."

Kai obeyed. "Thanks."

They stood surveying the endless river of cars and trucks on the multi-lane bridge.

The vehicles stood crammed together at odd angles, metal bent against metal and shattered glass everywhere, one massive collision stretching for a mile ahead.

A bloody, mutilated body sat inside the nearest car, a sedan that had crashed against the side barrier.

Kai staggered in shock. "Red sands!"

Val gave him a strange look, then walked past him to the car, his hand already reaching in his pocket for the tool. "Not used to dead bodies lying around, huh? Yeah, the sweepers are taking their time. But I'm not complaining." He used his elbow to knock down the cracked windshield, then stuck his arm in.

The tool looked like a small gun. He pressed the barrel against the corpse's neck and pulled the trigger. There were two fast clicks as the internal mechanism engaged and reset. Val scanned the digital display.

Kai's stomach twisted. "You... scrap human bodies?"

"Just taking a sample. Relax." Val glanced up at the empty sky, then started walking, picking his way between the ruined cars, heading down the bridge and toward the distant skyscrapers of the business district.

Kai followed, suddenly curious. "You mean DNA?" He'd done one meager online course on genetics, and was now racking his brain to remember any of it. "But what do you do with it?"

Val kept moving, reaching inside one car, then another, collecting more samples as he went. "Ever wanted to be someone else?"

Kai hesitated. Val still didn't know who he was. "Sure. Who hasn't?"

"That's right. And some people will pay good money for it."

"Okay. They want a new identity. I get that." Kai climbed over a half-crushed van, trying not to look at the bodies trapped by the seatbelts. A genetic sample could identify a person. He remembered that much from the course. But how could it make them into someone else? He was still stuck on that. "So how does it work?" he asked, feeling stupid.

"The sample is a marker."

"Of someone dead?"

"Of a name, address, online history. A whole package that's just become available," Val explained. "If you picked well, they're already the same body type as you. And any surgeon can give you a new face."

Kai's chest tightened. A memory surfaced. A green-eyed waitress reaching for his plate, her cheekbones a painful crimson after she overheard his harsh comment about the Mira look. And another memory, vague and uneasy, a connection made and lost too fast to grasp. "Hold on. But your genetics don't change. So if someone took another sample, they'd know the truth."

"Very good. That's why there's one more step. You get into the city database and swap the genetic records."

"Can *you* do that?"

Val shook his head. "No. I'm just a supplier. You need someone who can get past the firewalls and swap the files for you. A *swapper*. Big payoff. But if they catch you..." He shook his head again, his expression grim.

Kai's mind swung to his Agent, and the videos she'd told him to watch when he trained for the Race. Videos of events that were never broadcast on the show, events that officially never happened. But how did she get hold of them?

His pulse quickened, his mind seizing the possibility, no matter how thin. Was Emily a swapper? Was that why she'd left? To protect him from the risk? "Where? Where would I find someone like that?"

Up ahead, two lanes of the bridge split off and curved to the right, toward a mid-city sector, still a good mile away from the edge of the business district and the glass skyscrapers perpetually shrouded by smog.

Val shrugged. "The Boards. Where else?"

Kai hesitated. Apparently, the Boards were common

knowledge. Pushing for information at this point gave him away as an outsider. But something compelled him to tell the truth. "Never heard of them."

Val's eyes narrowed. "You never heard of the Boards? What, you grew up under a rock or something?"

Kai thought of his hometown being swallowed by the desert. "Something like that."

They walked in silence for a moment. Then Val spoke. "Ask Green when we get back. He'll show you."

Excitement surged through Kai. *When we get back.* So he was invited back. "Thanks. I will."

They headed down the two-lane bridge. The cars stood further apart here, making their passage easier and faster.

Until they reached a rough cement wall that blocked their way, its intent made clear by steel rods sticking out in all directions like knives and razor-sharp barbed wire strewn across the top. *Stay away.*

Cringing, Kai thought of the last day of the Race and the abandoned highway they ran on. He could see where the Network got the inspiration for the course.

A low buzz came from behind them, and they both spun toward the sound.

A huge hologram floated through the air along the highway, projected by a drone.

On the non-existent screen, a young man raced along a frozen river in a harsh winter landscape. The man's expression was fierce, and his feet were sleek prosthetic blades, curved upward and ending in sharp teeth.

Kai stared at the image, his heart pounding. He was looking at himself, on the first day of the Race, his face digitally altered just enough to be unrecognizable. And he already knew what came next.

"Fellow citizens of the Alliance..." Val mimicked the voice of the announcer. "Welcome to the most sadistic athletic competition on the planet."

In the hologram, the Runner rounded a bend at great speed—and plunged head first into the icy water.

But at the last moment, his arms shot forward. He wasn't falling. He was diving.

He kicked his legs, propelling himself deeper and deeper, further away from the cracked ice and the pale light that filtered through it. Until his hands touched the bottom of the river. He groped the frigid sand, searching for something. Then he found it, yanked it out, and kicked upward, back to the surface.

He climbed out, dripping with icy water, but satisfied. He lifted the object in his hand. It was a flexible tablet. He powered it on, and it started right away.

The Runner smiled with satisfaction. Then he rolled the tablet, slipped it into his pocket, and headed away, his blades cutting long strokes on the shimmering ice.

The scene faded to white, and the company name appeared.

3D Electronics.

Kai's near-drowning by Slayer's hand had been rewritten into a sleek commercial.

"It's all special effects, anyway," Val spat with disdain.

"Not all of it." Kai's limbs were frozen stiff and his skin burning with the memory of the icy water.

Val spun toward him. "Stop right there."

Kai turned. "What?" But he already knew.

"I'll be damned. I knew something was different about you." Val scanned him head to toe. "You're... him. You're... *Sand Runner.*"

A strange relief washed over Kai. Whatever happened, he didn't have to lie anymore. "Yeah. I'm Sand Runner. Or I *was.*"

"Sand Runner. In flesh and blood. I don't believe it." Val circled him. "What the hell are you doing here?"

Kai hesitated. "Good question. I'm still figuring it out myself."

Val chuckled. But there was no humor there. "What, you burned through all the cash already?"

Kai spoke cautiously. "It wasn't much to begin with."

"It never is, is it?" Val scowled. Then his expression changed. "Hold on... That's right. You didn't win. You gave it away. That last day of the Race, on the highway." He glanced around, remembering. "You helped *her* win. Venus."

"She deserved to win."

Val chuckled again, but this time the hard edge was gone. "If you say so." He looked away, his gaze moving over the distant horizon, his mind apparently on something else. "What about your Agent?"

It was like a stab to the chest. *His Agent.*

Kai swallowed. "What about her?"

"Doesn't your Agent earn a big, fat commission if you win?"

"My Agent didn't care about the money." Kai almost said *Emily*, but he bit his tongue.

"Is that right?" Val studied him. "Then what *did* she care about? Beating Slayer?"

Kai blinked in astonishment. "How do you know about that? It wasn't part of the official broadcast."

Val shifted to his good leg. "Word gets around."

They both fell silent.

Kai waited. Was that it? What happened now? Was he still welcome with the group?

As if in answer, Val pointed toward the cement barrier. "Come on. We better get going." He started climbing over the barbed wire. "Green's going to flip when he finds out who you are."

8
KAI

LEAH WAS WAITING for them when they returned. She ran to her brother and threw her arms around his neck, hugging him close. Then she pushed him away, her mouth trembling. "You scared me."

"I'm fine," Val protested gruffly, but he looked pleased.

Leah took a step toward Kai, as if to hug him too, but stopped herself, her cheeks a feverish red. "Thank you," she breathed, and hurried away.

The others came to greet them too. Young men and women crowded around Val, slapping him on the back or punching him in the shoulder.

"We thought we'd be digging you out, man."

"Glad you made it out of there in one piece."

They nodded at Kai, acknowledging him, and he nodded back.

*

"You're Sand Runner? *That* Sand Runner? For real?" Behind his thick lenses, Green's eyes were as big as saucers when Val finally told the group, later that night. "No way! No freaking way!" He was chewing on a candy bar and almost choked on it, laughing. His glasses slid from his nose, and he pushed them back up. "Sand Runner! Did you all hear that? Holy smokes!"

Kai endured it patiently, but the embarrassment burned under his skin. Green treated him like a star. More than that—like a hero. But Kai was neither.

Because if he was, why would Emily leave?

He had had several hours to ponder this when he and Val had walked down one dusty, crumbling street after another, weaving their way through an unfamiliar sector of the city back to the house. They made a few stops along the way, with Val climbing up dim staircases and disappearing inside silent apartments, the doors cracking open only long enough to let him in and then snapping shut, while Kai waited in the lobby, his back against the peeling walls and his thoughts stuck in an endless loop.

The Network only made him look like a hero—braver, stronger, and smarter than he really was. They created Sand Runner. But that wasn't Kai. He was only the raw material.

They had done the same for Slayer, constantly shining up his image, cutting out the scenes where his true darkness came through, changing him into someone he was not.

That's what editing was for. That's why the show aired six hours after it was recorded.

It had angered Kai at the time. But Slayer wasn't the only one who benefited from the lies. Sand Runner did as well.

The problem was, when the No Limits Race ended, Sand Runner was gone. It was just Kai again. Unedited and ordinary. No trace of a hero left.

No wonder Emily lost interest after only a few weeks.

It was Sand Runner who had won her over. What did Kai have to offer her?

Watching the gang at dinnertime only added to Kai's misery. The room was spacious enough for a small restaurant, with a tall, ornate fireplace, now boarded up to prevent the dust and smog from invading the house.

But the group sat elbow to elbow around several square tables pushed together, sharing food and stories like a big family, although Kai was pretty sure only Leah and Val were related by blood.

They weren't a sweet, loving family. Leah's display of affection definitely wasn't the norm. But they were still a family, a tough and loyal one, the bonds between them running deep and forged by all the struggles and hardship they had overcome together.

Sitting with them now, Kai had never felt so alone or so apart.

"Hey." Green elbowed him to get his attention. "Not exactly what you're used to, huh?" He indicated the 3D printed mush that was their meal.

Kai felt a pang of guilt. Food wasn't easy to come by. It was rude to waste it. "Are you kidding? This is all we eat back home." He loaded a spoonful and forced himself to swallow it. Then another. The trick was to get the food down without thinking about it.

"Yeah, I hear you." Green kept his spoon moving and his jaw working, but his expression was pained. "I can't wait for the harvest."

"The harvest?"

Across the table, a young man with a shaved head and burn scars all over his hands shot Green a sharp look.

Green got flustered. "Er... It's nothing." He cleared his throat. "Kai, this is Zip. Zip, this is—"

"I know who he is." Zip pushed off from the table. "I've got work to do." And he walked away, his plate in hand.

"Sorry about that," Green told Kai when Zip was safely out of the earshot. "He doesn't like strangers. But he's a good guy. We wouldn't last a day without him."

"It's cool. Don't worry about it," Kai said, but the nagging doubt was back. He wasn't one of them. He didn't belong here. "What work does he do?"

Green's eyes lit up. "He keeps us supplied with juice."

"Juice?"

"Electricity."

Kai was impressed. "How?"

Green cringed. "I... can't talk about it."

"It's fine." It was none of Kai's business anyway. But it reminded him of something else he wanted to know. "Hey. Val said you're an expert in the Boards. Can you give me a tour?"

Green sat up straight, beaming. "Val said that? For real?" He wolfed down the rest of his food, grabbed his plate, and got up. "Then let's go. Your tour starts right now."

They crossed from the dining room to the kitchen. The kitchen was a large, open space that still had an oven, a fridge, and a long stretch of countertops underneath tall cabinets. The food printer stood in the corner.

Green swiftly washed their plates in a tub of soapy water that sat in the sink, dried them with a frayed towel, and put them away. "Okay. Come on. I'm on the top floor."

The staircase had a metal handrail shaped like a snake's body. Kai passed his hand over the scales, worn smooth by human touch but their pattern still unmistakable. Something caught in his chest. He'd hated snakes ever since his parents' death. "How did you guys find this place?"

"We didn't find it. Ana invited us," Green said. "It's her house. Her parents got killed when the house was robbed."

"That's tough. I'm sorry." An image flashed through Kai's mind. Ana standing with Leah at the foot of the wreckage, her arm around Leah's shoulders, comforting and protecting her like a sister. He wanted to know more, but it felt like intruding, so he didn't ask.

The top floor had a low ceiling and a drop-down trap door leading to the attic above. There were only two rooms here.

Green pushed through the door on the right. "Here we are."

The room was so small and so cluttered, it looked like a storage closet. A long, wooden desk took up one entire wall. On the desk stood three large computer screens, multiple hard drives, speakers, keyboards, and other devices Kai had never seen, all mismatched and seriously outdated, with a tangle of cables connecting them in the back.

A bed stood along the opposite wall, but it was covered with stacks of books so tall they threatened to topple over. A thin mattress lay on the floor, covered with faded floral bedding. And on the walls, makeshift shelves buckled under more books and knickknacks of all sorts.

"Where did you get all this stuff?" Kai picked up a ceramic figure of a knight and inspected it.

"Careful with that." Green was next to him in a flash. He snatched the knight away and replaced him on the shelf.

Kai smiled. "You're a collector."

Green paled. "Not really." He crossed to his desk, dropped into the rotating chair, and spun a full circle. "Okay. Grab a seat." He flipped a switch and, one by one, the screens blinked to life.

Kai pulled up another chair and fixed his eyes on the largest screen, eager to get some answers. Someone had come out to watch him in the cage race and saved his life by posting on the Boards. And that someone was Emily. It had to be.

The Boards turned out to be a simple message forum, nothing but lines of black text on a white background with an occasional photo. The most recent post read: "*Men's boots needed, size 12. Bonus if waterproof.*" The next message said: "*Air masks available. Will deliver.*" The third message was only two words, "*Missing cat,*" and showed a blurry photo of a gray tabby.

Kai's disappointment must have shown on his face because Green hurriedly explained, "Hold on. One more step!" He clicked on an icon and typed several lines of code into a text box that appeared—and the Boards transformed, the background changing to black and text to white, and the lettering of the messages rearranging in front of their eyes. "Here we are!"

The new posts were very different, and each had a reply button underneath it.

The first post was for a job: "*Crew of 8 needed for urgent deliveries. Must know the business district.*"

The next message warned: "*Sectors 15, 16, and 17 scheduled for a sweep. Stay indoors.*"

But it was the third message that made Kai's pulse quicken. "*Man found in sector 7. Knife wounds. Stable but unconscious.*" A photo showed a bearded man lying on a mat, his eyes closed and his arm wrapped in bandages. "*Do you know him?*"

"Let me see that." Kai reached for the mouse and scrolled down the page.

Several more messages talked about injured men and women, calling for help with a medical emergency or urging anyone who knew them to come forward and take them home. There were no names and no dates. Only the reply button.

"The Boards belong to the people in the sectors." Green spoke with a solemn fervor. His lenses reflected the screen like two mirrors. "They're how we warn each other and help each other survive. They're our secret weapon."

Stubbornly, Kai kept scrolling down the page. The

message that had saved his life had to be there. And who else could have posted it if not Emily?

"You never know. One day a stranger may post on here and save *your* life," Green said.

A stranger.

Kai pushed the mouse away.

Green was right. The message that had saved him wasn't special. The Boards were full of them. Anybody could have posted it. This was just another dead end.

He was suddenly restless, the disappointment burning in his gut. "A secret weapon? You make it sound like it's an army going to war. But all I see is a bunch of people trying to make some money and stay out of trouble."

Green frowned behind his glasses. "That's true. The Boards aren't what they used to be since Syber left."

"Who's Syber?"

"Syber is a legend!" Green's voice was full of fervor again. "Nobody knows his true identity... or what happened to him. He didn't start the Boards, but he was the closest to a leader we had. He always signed his posts. If you saw his name, you knew the information was important. Everybody trusted him."

"But he left. Isn't that what you said?"

"He'll be back. I know he will." Green bit his lip. "We need him."

A bitter laugh rose in Kai's throat. This was too familiar. "Right. Good luck with that."

There was a sharp knock on the door, and Ana walked in. "Green, you got a minute? We need you."

Green was already on his feet. "Sure." He grabbed a piece of paper and scribbled all across it, then slapped it down in front of Kai. "Here. The login code. Practice it. Memorize it. You need to type it in fast, or it won't work." He glanced at the shelves. "And please don't break anything."

Kai raised his hands, palms out. "I won't touch a thing."

He was hoping for a smile from Ana, but she barely looked at him. "Come on, Green. Val's waiting."

After they left, Kai turned back to the screen, intending to search the Boards for the famed Syber. But the background was back to white, and the messages were about cats and shoes again. The system had logged him out.

Kai swore under his breath. Then studied Green's scribbled note and started typing.

9
EMILY

EMILY SAT ON a wide window seat, her arm touching the cool glass and her legs stretched in front of her.

Outside, drifting smog wove in and out of an unfamiliar sector of the city, the setting sun giving it an ugly, orange cast.

From her high vantage point—at least twenty floors up—she could see a highway in the distance. A long stretch of the overpass had collapsed. A flock of sweeper drones were working their way through the wreckage, identifying the bodies, verifying and recording the deaths, and then incinerating the cars with high-intensity lasers.

Most of the deceased would enter the final, inactive stage of their existence, as data points on a city server. But some would enjoy a reincarnation of sorts, their digital identities hacked, stolen, and sold to those who needed a fresh start and didn't mind the risk.

Emily knew all about that.

Sighing, she looked down at the tablet in her lap, and her hands moved over the touchscreen. She was working on the database, racing to crack open a folder, any folder, before the whole structure rearranged again.

The apartment was dead silent. A layer of dust covered the floors and a few pieces of furniture left behind by the last occupant. The whole floor of the building was abandoned, as were several floors below it.

People still lived in the apartments on the lower levels, but apparently no one had the energy or the desire to climb up and down the stairs.

All of this suited Emily just fine. She didn't plan to stay here long, anyway.

A small window in the corner of her screen streamed live news, and she glanced at it from time to time. She had set it to find and play any news stories about Hollenbach or BioPrintex. But at the moment, all the bots were picking up was the footage of new recruits arriving at the Training Center. Preparations for the Eleventh Global No Limits Race were underway.

Emily hit a key, and the window shrunk to a small tile. She didn't want to think about the Race right now. It brought back too many memories, and she needed to focus.

On the screen, the structure stretched and divided, whole segments breaking off, only to collide and merge again. Each folder, barely a voxel in size at this scale, was protected with its own encryption. And inside the folders was information Emily had already risked more than one life to acquire...

She gritted her teeth and focused harder. She could handle the encryption. She had the keys. The problem was getting the structure to collapse into a stable pattern.

A key wasn't useful if she couldn't get hold of a door.

Then suddenly—she had it.

It happened fast, her fingers executing the action almost on their own.

The system glitched—and a folder flew at her, separate from the rest.

She snatched it, dragged it, locked it in place.

Once it was motionless, cracking the encryption was easy. The folder sprang open, revealing a list of files, all beginning with the same string of letters and numbers. A patient ID.

Emily shivered. She had no idea what happened—she just got lucky. But now she was one step closer.

She opened file after file, scanning the contents. There were medical test results, genetic analyses, endless biotech data. All important evidence, but not specific enough. No legal or financial documents, which must have been stored in a separate folder for added security. All in all, standard documentation for a patient undergoing a premium clinical procedure. Nothing suspicious. Nothing out of the ordinary.

Until she spotted a video file. She hesitated, then hit the play key.

A patient lay on an operating table, his chest cavity held open with metal braces and hooked up to drainage pipes, while a dozen robotic arms performed a heart surgery. With cold precision, the biological heart was removed, and a new one readied to put in its place.

A sleek, artificial model with the name clearly visible.

Titan SI 200.

Emily stopped the clip and stared at the frame, her body suddenly cold.

The procedure in the video may have looked like a standard heart transplant, but she knew better. There was nothing standard about the device or about the terms on which a patient was allowed to use it.

She had known about Falcon's plan for a few years, ever since her brief stunt working at 3D Electronics. But seeing it put into practice still came as a shock.

It was all happening too fast. She needed more time, more evidence. Data from a single patient wasn't nearly enough, and that's all she had so far.

Unless... she could locate that patient and get them to talk to her.

Emily closed the video clip and got to work.

All of the files in the folder used the patient ID

instead of the person's name, and looking for a genetic match in online databases would take too long. But after another hour of searching through the files and poring over technical descriptions and data tables, she found what she needed. Detailed blood work, a list of hospital visits with times and locations, an emergency contact. Enough for her bots to piece together the person's identity.

Sylvia Wagner, age 27, resident of sector 2.

"Got you."

A professional profile photo showed a blond woman with intelligent eyes. She wore a sharp business suit and radiated confidence. According to her profile page, she was an asset analyst at one of the largest financial management firms in the city. An image search showed her at upscale gallery openings and dining in expensive, real-food restaurants. Her luxury condo, expensively furnished and with original art painted directly on the walls, was featured on a trendy blog.

Judging by the information online, Sylvia Wagner had not a care in the world.

But unease gnawed at Emily. Something wasn't right. She had to dig deeper.

And indeed, a more careful search revealed Sylvia no longer worked at the firm, her name absent from the employee directory. A brief news article, dated from two weeks prior, helped shed light on the matter. A recent upgrade in the financial analysis AI platform had made Sylvia's job obsolete and her career prospects null. Her apartment, easily recognizable thanks to the wall art, was already listed for sale.

Sylvia was broke.

"No," Emily breathed in disbelief, a dark foreboding pushing in. What were the chances? The first patient file she ever laid her hands on, and she could already be too late.

"Where are you, Sylvia? I need to find you."

Incredibly, Sylvia was still on social media, and her last post, only minutes old, gave away her location. She was attending another gallery opening. A photo showed her with a glass of champagne. She was raising a toast, her lips stretched in a smile. But her eyes looked scared and desperate. She was out of options, and she knew it.

Emily hurriedly got up and slipped the tablet into her backpack, next to Kai's silver jacket that lay rolled on the bottom. Then she put on her long black coat, shrugged on the pack, and was on her way.

Outside, it was already night. The business district was visible in the distance. The Training Center and other skyscrapers stood brightly lit against the dark, starless sky. The smog blurred their outlines and swallowed their rooftops.

Emily slipped on her mask, lifted her hood, and headed in that direction.

Drones and hover cabs passed overhead, but otherwise the streets were empty and eerily quiet. The only sound was the hum and hiss of the powerful air purification systems inside the walls. People in the business district didn't venture outside if they could help it. Everything they needed was indoors, including fresh air.

The building complex ahead held a shopping mall and entertainment center. Emily crossed to a side entrance. The heavy double doors slid open reluctantly, allowing her in.

She breathed with relief. Most of the patrons used skywalks that connected the complex directly with a dozen luxury condo buildings that surrounded it or arrived by hover cabs which landed on the roof.

Emily lowered her hood, slipped off her face mask, and stepped onto an escalator. In moments, she was inside a posh shopping mall, surrounded by dizzying digital displays and holographic ads. People hurried past her, but most were too intent on their electronic devices to even notice her.

Good. The last thing she needed was to attract any attention.

The gallery was on the top level of the mall. The doors were wide open and welcoming, but matching red lights blinked on the door frame. An electronic ticket was required to enter.

Emily hesitated, then righted her backpack and marched through the door. The lights blinked green as she passed.

She smiled. Kai's jacket, a gift from Falcon, came in handy. It not only blocked wireless transmission, which meant she couldn't be tracked, but also served as a universal electronic ID.

Inside the gallery, a river of people flowed leisurely through a series of spacious, interconnected rooms, chatting and sipping champagne as they admired large digital images on the walls. The lights were dimmed, and strange string music vibrated in the air.

Emily walked from room to room, searching for the bearer of the Titan SI 200 heart.

Sylvia was in the last room. She wore a long black dress and stood alone, engrossed in the study of an image, her silhouette outlined by the light. Her fingers held an empty champagne glass.

Emily started toward her. Then her eyes went to the art on the wall, and she froze.

A cloud of oversized insects filled the frame, their wings beating so slowly they seemed to float in the air, nearly motionless. They all faced the camera, their heads alien and terrifying up close.

It took Emily a moment to remember where she'd seen the insect before. Venus's interview during last year's Race. Venus had bitten into the insect on camera, triggering a shockwave of awe and solidarity in millions of poor and desperate people around the globe. Even the wealthy were impressed. The insect became the hottest trend in art and fashion.

A gasp of pain pulled her back.

Sylvia shuddered, her silhouette bent, shoulders curling forward. The champagne glass sailed from her fingers and shattered on the floor.

Emily rushed to her side. "Sylvia."

Sylvia stared at her with wide eyes, her face drained of color. Her hands fluttered to her chest. "Who—who are you? Are you—are you one of them?"

"No, I'm not," Emily assured her. "I'm a friend. I want to help you."

"Help me?" A spasm twisted Sylvia's face, and she clawed at her throat and chest. Her breath was short and ragged. "You—you have the money?"

Emily felt a stab of panic. "I don't." So her suspicion was right. Sylvia couldn't make the payments anymore. "But there must be another way. I know someone—"

But Sylvia wasn't listening. Another shudder went through her, more powerful than before, and she sank to her knees. She clawed at the front of her dress until it tore open, exposing a metal insert with a brightly lit patient ID above her left breast. "It... hurts," Sylvia moaned.

Emily reached for the girl's hand. "Hang in there. It'll pass. It's just a warning." She tried to sound confident. "You're valuable to them. They need the data." But even as she said it, she knew it was a lie. It wasn't a research study anymore. It was a business with a very expensive product and huge profit margins. Sylvia had been valuable only as long as she had been a paying customer.

By now, the patrons formed a half-circle around

them, gawking and whispering.

"What's wrong with her?"

"She needs a doctor!"

"Somebody call an ambulance!"

Sylvia's eyes, full of terror, locked on Emily's face. "No ambulance. Please..." Then she sighed, her body relaxing and her eyes closing. The pain was gone.

Hope surged through Emily. Maybe it really was just a warning. But one glance at the metal insert on Sylvia's chest, and her hope turned into grief. The patient ID, brightly lit a moment ago, now turned dark. She felt for Sylvia's pulse and found none.

The girl lying on the floor next to her was dead.

Emily stared, numb with shock. An overwhelming sadness filled her. "I'm sorry," she whispered.

The sound of heavy footsteps roused her. Several men were heading her way.

"Let us through," a gruff voice demanded.

"Are you the medics?" a patron asked.

"Out of the way," was the only answer.

These were no medics.

Emily was on her feet at once. She slipped into the crowd and out of view not a moment too soon.

But she couldn't bring herself to leave. She watched from the back as two men lifted Sylvia's body onto a stretcher while a third worked on his tablet. "The signal is back. No idea what happened." And then, a minute later, "Okay. We've got all we need. Let's go."

The crowd parted without a word to let them pass. Nobody stopped them. Nobody questioned why no medical care was given or even attempted.

Emily's eyes stung, but the tears didn't fall, the sadness giving way to anger and resolve.

Falcon would *not* get away with this. She wouldn't let him. People had to know.

10
KAI

KAI SAT at a work table, bent low over a circuit board that he was trying to deconstruct without burning off his fingers or breaking the whole thing. There were three steps. First, he used a heat gun to heat the board. That caused some parts to fall right off. Then he worked with tweezers to remove the more stubborn parts. They fell on a cloth that lay in front of him. The last step was sorting the miniature components into a row of bins in the middle of the table.

Two other people worked next to him. The girl, Riko, wielded a soldering iron to remove the parts from large boards, which lay in a pile next to her. The guy, called Hans, used a pocket knife to pry electric circuits out of lightbulbs and then take them apart. Each had a cloth in front of them too, but they sorted the parts into the bins right away.

Kai glanced up at them often. Riko and Hans both worked in silence, and they were fast and efficient. They made the task look easy. But it wasn't. And the silence weighed on him.

"How's it going?" Green appeared next to him.

Just this morning, Kai had asked Green for a job, and Green had considered for a moment and then brought him to the workroom and showed him what to do.

The task had seemed odd at first, as if Kai was doing things backward. He thought of Ron, his friend from home. Being a mechanic, Ron used the same tools. Only he built things with them instead of taking things apart. It had never occurred to Kai that you could use the same tool to build or destroy. It was a strange thought.

What Kai really wanted was to go on another job with Val.

He saw the red-haired man talking to the others, their faces serious and intent. He could tell they were planning something. But the conversation always stopped when Kai moved closer. They still didn't trust him, and he couldn't blame them.

Green pushed his thick glasses higher on his nose and squinted at the small pile of parts on Kai's cloth. "Okay. You can start sorting them now."

Riko looked up and pushed one bin toward Kai. "The capacitors go in here."

Kai peered inside the bin, then searched his pile for similar parts. Found one. "Like this one?"

Hans squinted at it and shook his head. "Nope. That's an inductor. They go in here." He pushed another bin toward Kai.

"An inductor. Got it." Kai studied the part, determined to commit it to memory.

Green leaned closer. "Don't listen to them. They're messing with you. It's a transistor." He pulled a third bin toward Kai.

Kai stopped and looked at them. The corners of Green's mouth twitched. Riko and Hans were barely keeping straight faces themselves.

"Okay. Glad you guys are having fun." Kai wasn't thrilled about being the butt of their jokes. But it was only fair. He had no clue what he was doing. "Now are you going to teach me or not?"

They did.

Within a few days, he could take apart any circuit board and correctly sort the parts. He also explored the workroom, learning to use all the tools he could find.

Once he got the basics, Riko and Hans showed him how to build simple circuits too. It was a thrill to solder the tiny parts onto a board, weave wires between them, and suddenly end up with a circuit that did something useful, even if that something was as ordinary as making a light blink or an alarm sound. And the more he learned, the more his curiosity grew.

"What else can we build?" was his constant question to Riko and Hans.

Now that he paid attention, he saw electronic circuits everywhere, and he marveled at them. They were in all machines and devices. When the circuits were intact, the machine worked. But break even one, and you could break the whole machine.

He inspected his own prosthetic feet in wonder. What did the circuits inside look like? He vaguely remembered the complicated diagrams Neen pulled up on her computer. Even the most complicated circuits he built with Riko and Hans paled in comparison. And Neen had designed and built them herself.

He had a new respect for his Print Maker. He also had a lot of questions, but they would have to wait until he saw her again.

Meanwhile, Kai's new temporary home was like a well-functioning device. All around him was activity and purpose. Everyone had things to do, tasks they were responsible for, and they went about their work with quiet diligence and without friction.

When Kai wasn't in the workroom with Riko and Hans, or helping out with other jobs, he logged into the Boards and studied the messages.

He had been searching for the message that saved his life, but he never found it. Neither did he see any messages signed by Syber. The archive looked like it stretched back for years, but there were no dates, and as Green admitted, messages were often erased after their usefulness had passed. Although you could only delete your own messages and no one else's.

He spent a whole night glued to Green's computer and still came up empty-handed.

It was a strange night, anyway, and he wasn't eager to repeat it. Several times, he found he wasn't on the Boards anymore, but instead searching for Emily on the broad internet, even though he didn't remember deciding to do that.

He would type her name, *Emily Starr*, then her nickname, *Em*, and finally, random things he recalled her saying.

I'm here, Kai.

I don't care if you like me or hate me.

What if it doesn't pay off?

But when the search engine returned the results, he hardly looked at them. He didn't really expect to find anything useful. Most of the results made no sense, anyway. He was just killing time. He had searched everywhere and found no trace of Emily, nothing to point him in her direction. Now he was stuck.

After that, Kai stayed away from the Boards and the internet. He preferred the workroom. There, he could keep his mind busy with work, and the time passed faster.

One day Leah walked in. "Hi, guys."

Kai was using a soldering iron to melt parts off a large circuit board. Across the table from him, Rika, Hans, and Green worked with tweezers. They all looked up at her. "Hi."

Leah sat down next to Kai. She was holding a small circuit with a wire sticking out. She pointed to Kai's soldering iron. "Mind if I borrow that for a second?"

"Sure." He offered it to her. "But be careful. It's very

hot."

Riko smirked, and Green's eyebrows went up.

Leah smiled, a spark of mischief in her eyes. "Good to know." Then she deftly plucked the soldering iron from Kai's fingers and got to work.

Kai had watched Ron, and now Riko and Hans, handle a soldering iron a hundred times, but he'd never seen anything like the way the iron danced in Leah's fingers, fast and graceful. A moment later, she handed it back. "Thanks. You were right. It's very hot."

Kai smiled. "Right. So what are you building?"

"More like fixing." Leah laughed. "It's for the irrigation system. The switch jams all the time."

Green paled and quickly leaned against the table. "Hey, Kai. You could try heating the board from the back. So the parts won't stick."

It was a lame attempt to distract him, and Kai saw right through it. Didn't Green mention a harvest once, only to earn a glare from Zip?

"Irrigation system? What's that about?" he asked Leah.

Leah laughed. "Do you know another way to farm without rain?" She picked up her circuit and turned to the door.

Green interjected again, really nervous now. "See here? You hold the board like this—"

But Kai's eyes were on Leah. Farm without rain? So the plants were inside the house. He had to see it.

"Here, you do it!" He stuck the soldering iron into Green's outstretched hand and jumped to his feet. "Leah, wait! Can I come with you?"

She smiled at him from the door. There was no hesitation there. "Of course. If you want." She let Kai catch up, and they walked out of the workroom together.

"Oh, man." Green moaned behind them.

Leah rolled her eyes. “Don’t mind him.”

But Kai was suddenly worried. “Are you going to get in trouble? I mean, for showing me the farm?”

Leah laughed again. They were walking up the stairs, and she was a little out of breath. “I won’t get in trouble. Don’t worry. And we call it a greenhouse, not a farm.”

“Fine, a greenhouse. But your brother wants to keep it a secret, right?” Kai pressed. “That’s why Green is so nervous?”

Leah sighed, pushing her hair from her face. “A secret from strangers, yes. But you’re not a stranger. I know we can trust you,” she said simply.

“Yeah. You can trust me.” He should be flattered by her declaration, but instead, it made him uneasy. “But that doesn’t mean you should trust everyone. Especially if you have something other people want, something valuable. It’s better to be cautious than risk losing it.”

“Now you sound like Val!” Leah threw him a sideways glance as they turned into the second-floor hallway.

“Maybe he’s right.”

Leah shook her head. “I love my brother, and he’s a good leader. But he always expects the worst of people.” She paused in front of a wide, stained-glass door and turned to Kai, meeting his gaze. “Well, I would rather trust someone and be wrong than push someone away and lose a friend. So here’s the greenhouse.”

And with that, she pushed the door open, and they went in.

Kai took two steps and stopped, his chest tight. A memory swept through him, transporting him to a different time and place, to a different girl.

Suddenly, he was in the indoor garden in the Training Center with Emily, on their first date. The sensations crowded in, taking his breath away. Emily’s turned head, the pencil moving in her fingers as she sketched, her eyes meeting his gaze. The warmth of her skin when he took her hand in his, the sweetness of her mouth when he pulled her close and kissed her.

I'm still your Agent first.

And I'm still your Runner.

He could remember it all so vividly it hurt.

Without knowing what he was doing, Kai hurried along the narrow path, his heart pounding. He passed Leah and kept going. The plants were too green, too lush. They weren't right. He had to find the desert. Emily was waiting for him there.

Kai got to the end of the garden and stared at the wall, confused and disappointed, as if waking from a dream. He had practically run the last part, following the girl who wasn't there.

Leah caught up with him, worry on her face. "Kai, what's wrong? Are you okay?"

He looked at her as if he'd never seen her before. "What?" It came out harsh. "Sorry. I'm fine. It's... nothing."

Leah studied him with sad, knowing eyes. "It's alright. You don't have to explain. I understand."

Kai wouldn't know how to explain anyway. He pointed at the circuit in Leah's fingers, eager to change the subject. "So where does this thing go?"

She glanced down as if she just remembered it. "Oh yeah. I better put this back before we have a lake." She hurried to the far corner of the room, where a portion of the pipe was wrapped in a rag and plastic to control the leak.

Kai followed close behind. "Can I help?"

But Leah didn't need his help. The job done, she was just getting up and brushing the dirt off her knees when Green burst in the door, startling them both. "Guys, come on! You have to see it! Downstairs!"

He turned around and rushed back out without waiting for a response.

Kai and Leah looked at each other, then hurried after him.

11
KAI

WHEN KAI AND LEAH got downstairs, the group was gathered in front of the large television in the living room.

With a high ceiling, tall windows, and ornate moldings on the walls, it must have been an airy and elegant room once. But now, with the windows boarded up and plain lightbulbs as the only source of illumination, it resembled a cave.

Riko, Hans, and Ana sat on a long sofa. Others sat in the heavy armchairs or on the carpet. Val was leaning against the wall.

One glance at the screen, and every muscle in Kai's body tensed.

Looking straight at him were the catlike green eyes of Meghan Moore, the host of the official broadcast of the Race.

"And now, the moment you've all been waiting for, and the start of a new era in the most extreme athletic competition on the planet." Meghan gave a brilliant smile, her voice swelling with emotion. "Fellow citizens of the Alliance, I give you—the first Runner to qualify for the Eleventh Global No Limits Race." She turned, and the camera pulled away, revealing her new co-host, an athletic-looking man, and the giant screen lighting up behind them. "Meet—"

But Meghan's voice turned into grating static, while

the image wavered and stretched, parts of it splintering into a frozen mosaic.

There was a universal groan of protest in the room. "Nooo! Come on!"

Green rushed to the television, tripping over people's legs in the dim light. But Zip beat him to it. "I've got it, I've got it." He opened the control panel and started fiddling with the settings.

The sound was still static, but the image returned, and it needed no commentary.

Kai watched transfixed. He already knew what was coming.

On the screen, a young man with raven black hair sprinted on a hard ground that cracked and crumbled in his wake, his bare feet gradually transforming until they were sleek prosthetic blades.

But he kept sprinting. It wasn't over yet. There was more to come.

Kai stared at the screen, a terrible suspicion rising in him.

The static rose in pitch, grating and unpleasant.

"Zip! The sound! Hurry up!" someone urged.

"Hey, you want to do it?" Zip snapped.

The image wavered again, then stabilized.

The raven-haired man sprinted on his prostheses, his legs pumping, his arms slicing the air. But something was happening again. His left arm was also changing... until it became a powerful robotic gripper.

There was a collective gasp of shock.

Kai stood frozen and mute, his mind refusing to accept what he saw.

The metallic fingers snatched a rock off the ground and crushed it to dust. Then the camera zoomed in on the Runner's wrist, and the company logo, engraved in the metal, filled the screen.

3D Electronics.

Kai staggered. His hands clenched into fists as a memory slammed into him. Falcon's cold, appraising eyes when he visited Kai after the surgery. Taking the legs wasn't enough? Now Falcon wanted an arm too?

"You greedy bastard," Kai muttered.

He turned and met Val's eyes.

He couldn't tell if the man heard him or not. But judging by the look on his face, they were on the same page. Val looked ready for murder.

Green pushed his way to the control panel, his thick lenses flashing with the reflected glow of the screen. "Zip, let me try."

Zip frowned at him, irritated. "What are *you* going to do?" But he stepped aside.

Green pushed his glasses up his nose and got to work.

Meghan's face filled the screen again, and, incredibly, the sound returned. "We'll be right back after these important messages. So don't go anywhere. You won't want to miss this."

"Good job, Green!" Riko hooted, and a few people laughed and clapped. Green bowed.

But a hush fell over the room when the screen turned dark and a stirring music filled the air. The commercial had started.

"Have you ever been sick or injured? Forced to give up your dreams because a physical infirmity got in the way? Dreading what the future will bring?" a warm voice inquired while the darkness shifted and moved, suggesting violent accidents, intense suffering, and death without actually displaying any of them. "Now you can put it all behind you."

Kai couldn't help but think of Val, with his limp, and Green, nearly blind without his glasses. And of Emily when he first met her. There was something callous and malicious about the commercial, something that put him on edge, although he couldn't explain what it was.

On the screen, a burst of sunlight dispersed the darkness. Now silhouettes of athletes exercising and couples embracing animated the picture, while the music soared, vigorous and triumphant. "Live *two hundred years* in perfect health," the voice urged emphatically, "with ground-breaking, self-powering and self-monitoring replacement organs..." A line of sleek, expensive-looking devices appeared, and underneath them, the company name, glowing like gold. "Only from 3D Electronics."

Abruptly, the television turned off.

Val tossed the remote away, his expression dark and his voice rough and impatient. "Alright. Enough of this. We have work to do."

Instantly, there was movement. People getting to their feet. Grabbing their jackets and backpacks, which they had kept nearby in readiness. They formed a circle around Val.

Green threw one last look at the screen, sad to miss whatever was coming, then joined in.

Kai watched them. It was a big group, so it had to be a big job. And he wanted in.

He walked up to Val. "Do you have room for one more?"

A few people exchanged looks. Something was up.

Val studied him. "You better sit this one out. You won't like it."

"Come on. I'm sick of sitting. I want to come."

Val frowned, then shrugged. "Suit yourself. But don't tell me I didn't warn you." He turned to the door.

Leah walked up to Kai. "Take this. You'll need it." She handed him a face mask.

"Thanks." Kai took it. "You're not coming?"

Leah glanced at Val, then shook her head. She looked very pale. "No." Then she added, "take care of yourself."

"You too," Kai said. It just slipped out.

She smiled. "Me? What can happen to me? I'm staying right here." She glanced at Ana, who stood nearby, apart from the group. It looked like the two of them were the only ones staying behind.

Kai looked at Ana and met with a sharp, hostile gaze. Val may not have accepted him into the group, but he at least tolerated him. But Ana still held some kind of grudge against him, although Kai had no idea why. There was something about her that sent a chill down his spine.

Val spoke. "Okay. Let's get moving, everyone. Stay sharp. If we have to split up, you know where to go."

The group filed out the door. Once in the street, they moved fast, with Val in the lead, propelled by the same shared purpose as before.

Kai kept pace but stayed in the back. His thoughts drifted to the Race and the black-haired Runner with a gripper for a hand.

Last year, the price to compete was two feet. That's what Kai had paid. This year, the price had increased to include an arm. What would it be next year, or ten years from now? And would there still be recruits willing to pay it?

He remembered Falcon's demonstration of his own prosthetic hand. The wrist turning in a continuous rotation, the pressure of a finger enough to crack a cement wall. Now he wondered how much of Falcon was still flesh and bone and how much had been augmented with the devices coming out of his own research labs.

But there was a difference. Falcon had a choice. At least Kai thought so. Would all the recruits have the same choice?

And what about accident victims who couldn't afford the augmentations? Or people who were born different and preferred to stay that way? Could they still choose for themselves, or would people like Falcon dictate their options?

The group walked in silence, taking a new direction from the one they had followed last time. Soon, the cracked sidewalks and crumbling walls became unfamiliar again. The air tasted sharp.

Kai coughed. Val shot him a look over his shoulder. Then he produced a mask and put it on.

The others followed suit. Kai did as well. It was a relief.

Green turned and waited for him until they walked side by side. "You know what? You're alright. You're not like the other Runners."

"The *other* Runners?" Kai looked at him. "How many Runners do you know?"

Green flushed. Smog had coated his glasses, and he rubbed the lenses clean without taking them off. "Well. None... personally. But I've heard the stories."

"The stories?"

"Yeah, you know. How after they've been in the Race, they think they're better than the rest of us. How they never go back to see their families and friends. Just disappear and nobody ever hears from them again."

Kai frowned. "Where did you hear that? On the Boards?"

Green shook his head. "No. Not on the Boards. Just... around."

"Around, huh?"

So there were lies on both sides, as if someone deliberately tried to stir suspicion and hostility between the Runners and their fans. Kai had been fed lies too. That people hated him, that his life would be in danger if he ever revealed who he was.

None of it was true, at least so far.

"Well, don't believe everything you hear," he told Green. "I went back to see my friends. And I know other

Runners did as well. Venus and Beast did too, I think."

"*Venus.* Wow," Green said in a dreamy voice. "I forgot you knew her. Lucky you." Then for some reason, he stuck his hand into his pocket and produced two candy bars. He offered one to Kai. "Here. Technically, half of them are yours."

Kai totally forgot about their loot from the wrecked van. "Thanks. But you keep them."

Green blinked. "You sure? Okay." He tore the wrapper off, slipped the bar under his mask, and took a bite. He finished it in two hurried bites and adjusted his mask.

Kai gave him a questioning look.

Green pointed up.

A drone glided over the street up ahead. The buildings were in better shape here, and hover cabs passed overhead. They had to be near the business center. This was a police drone.

Kai hadn't seen a police drone in a while. There were no police in the poor sectors. Someone in power had decided that the people who lived there should fend for themselves and solve their own problems. But here, in the business center, people had enough money to pay for security.

The group kept walking. They turned into a narrow alley and followed it to the end. Then they emerged into a wide street.

Here they picked up their pace.

Kai looked up, and once more, memories flooded in.

In front of them, less than ten blocks away, was the familiar massive structure, the top floors disappearing into the smog that covered the sky.

They were heading for the Training Center.

12
KAI

KAI STOPPED, staring at the mammoth structure of the Training Center rising ahead. So this is why Val had warned him. But what business brought them here?

Green gestured to Kai, urging him on. They had to keep moving.

The group turned into a side street and approached a heavy gate. To Kai's surprise, the gate opened to admit them, and they descended into an underground structure. It stretched a dozen floors down like a vertical maze. Val led them past a row of large machines connected by a system of pipes and down a corridor ending in a series of tall lockers.

One by one, the lockers clicked open as they approached. As with the gate, their arrival was anticipated.

Like on cue, a screen positioned by the first locker blinked on, and a man's face appeared.

Kai stared at the face on the screen—one he'd hoped to never see again.

"What's up, doc?" Val said, a hint of mockery in his voice.

The man was the surgeon who had operated on Kai before the Race.

"Keep the cases upright at all times. The items are fragile and will be destroyed if the cases are compromised in any way. Payment after confirmed delivery."

"We've done this before. We know the drill." Val pulled open the nearest locker. There was a hiss, and cold air filled the space. "You go take care of your *patients*."

There were a few smirks from the group.

On the screen, the doctor pursed his lips, clearly irked by the lack of respect. "You have one hour."

And the screen blinked off.

Val backed up into the locker, reaching for the object stored inside it. He stepped away, carrying a tall backpack. Wide padded arm straps supported a tall and narrow back. The cargo inside it had straight, sharp edges, and it was clearly heavy, judging by the look of effort and concentration on Val's face. He put his weight on his bad leg and winced, grabbing the locker door to keep himself from falling. A hum of electronic equipment came from inside the pack.

The location, the timing, the shape of the backpacks. It all came together in a snap.

Kai swallowed. "What's inside?"

Val threw him a look. Then signaled to Green. "Let him see it."

Green unzipped the top of the backpack, revealing a transparent layer underneath it, which secured the cargo in place.

A human arm floated in a glass tank, suspended from a net of tubes and wires. A heavy base contained the computer that controlled the bio-support system.

Kai took a step back. "Red sands."

The arm was lean and muscular, with a strong wrist and long fingers. Had it belonged to the Runner they saw on the broadcast? Maybe, maybe not. So close to the official start of the Race, dozens of recruits probably underwent the amputation every day, although most would never qualify for the competition. The arm could have belonged to any of them.

Val nodded to Green, and he zipped the protective layer back up.

Val turned to Kai. "I told you you wouldn't like it. Now we've got to go."

The group had split into teams of two. Hans and Riko. Karim and Ivy. Marco and Nolan. Zip and Green. One person carrying the backpack, the other keeping an eye on things.

The pairs nodded to Val and took off. They were splitting up from here on. Each package was to be delivered to a different address.

"You come with me," Val told Kai, and they headed back past the row of machines. They exited the gate and headed down the street. Kai looked around, but the others were already out of sight.

They walked in silence. Kai was still processing what he saw. "So... you deliver to the Collectors," he finally said.

"I deliver to whoever pays enough to make it worth my time," Val said coldly.

"Have you met any of them?" Kai asked.

Val threw him a look. "No. And I don't intend to. I deliver the goods and get paid. That's it."

But Kai couldn't help but be curious about the Collectors. Ever since he had first heard of them, he had been shocked and sickened by the idea.

What monster would purchase a human limb, and then keep it alive and on display? And yet, that's what the bio-support tanks were designed to do. First, to maintain a basic level of physiological function. And second, to be looked at, studied, admired from all angles.

It all came back to him. The horror stories he heard about the Collectors and their auctions.

He had had no personal experience with them. He had thought at one point that Peter Falcon, his Sponsor in the Race, was one. Falcon had acquired Kai's amputated feet and later presented them to Kai as a gift, with an offer to reattach them after the competition was over. Except it wasn't a gift—it was a test. To see if Kai would cling to his natural human limbs, which Falcon regarded as hopelessly inferior, or embrace the superior ones that Falcon had given him. Kai saw through it and passed the test.

Falcon was pleased and let him have his amputated feet back anyway. He was not a Collector and never really cared about them.

Kai had lied to Falcon about not wanting his feet reattached. But once he had them in his possession, he discovered an even better use for them. With Andy's help, the feet were auctioned off, and the money paid for Emily's surgery.

Emily.

The thought of her stung. Where was she right now? Would he ever see her again?

Val set a fast pace. They had a deadline, and an hour wasn't much time to travel on foot in the city. But now he was struggling. The backpack was heavy, too heavy for his bad leg, and he could barely walk, even on the flat surface. When they had to climb a series of steps, his jaw clenched in pain.

"You okay?" Kai asked.

Val was breathing hard. He tore off his mask and stuffed it into his pocket. "I'm fine. Just can't breathe with this damn thing on."

But his limp was slowing them down. They both knew it. Val was simply too proud to admit a weakness, too stubborn to ask for help.

Finally, Kai caught his arm, stopping him. "Come on, man," he said. "You've done enough. It's my turn. Let me carry it."

Val frowned at him. "All right."

When he transferred the backpack over, Kai nearly fell backward. "Red sands." But he righted himself, his prosthetic feet adjusting to the new task. "Okay. I'm good. I've got it."

Val put his mask back on, and they picked up the pace. They were almost out of time.

Val led them into an alley that ran alongside a luxury apartment building. A hovercraft was already waiting. Next to it stood two large men with stun guns strapped to their thighs.

"Cutting it close," the taller one said.

The other one stepped behind Kai and unzipped the cover of the backpack, peering inside. He nodded to the first man, then stepped closer, ready to relieve Kai of his load. "Okay. Easy does it."

But Kai took a step back. It wasn't planned. It was just a wild idea that popped into his head. "I want to deliver it in person."

The taller man narrowed his eyes, his movements suddenly slow and menacing. "I'm afraid not. Just hand it over, and we can go our separate ways."

"Who's your boss?" Kai pressed. "I want to meet him."

Val grabbed Kai's arm. "What are you doing?" He glared at Kai over his mask. "You heard him. Give him the backpack, and let's get out of here."

The tall man was about to speak again but stopped, his head cocked as if he was listening.

Kai recognized the earring the man wore. It was a communication link. He had worn one just like it in the Race. He waited.

The tall man nodded to the air. "Yes, sir. Understood." Then he turned to Kai. "My boss says you can come up. But only you. And the mask has to come off."

Morbid excitement shot through Kai. He was about to meet a Collector face to face. "Works for me." He yanked the mask off his face and stuck it in his pocket.

"What the hell are you doing?" Val glared at him. "Are you crazy?"

"Maybe." It probably *was* crazy. But he had made up his mind.

The shorter man again reached for Kai's backpack, and this time Kai let him take it. The man lifted it easily and carefully deposited it into the deep trunk of the hovercraft that had slid open.

The taller man stepped forward and pressed something into Kai's hand. It was a thick roll of cash. Kai handed it to Val. "Here. Take it. I'll see you."

Val shook his head. Then he took the money, turned, and walked away.

Kai got in the hovercraft, and it started rising, straight up and fast, like an elevator. Passing all the floors, then the roof of the building, until there was only open air.

The Collector lived in an airborne loft.

Kai stared at the structure in awe. It appeared to float in the air above the building. But then he saw the support beams, transparent and barely visible.

It was 3D printing again. It made possible what no other building technology could accomplish. But the design was also highly practical for someone who valued their privacy and security. The only way to reach the loft—or to depart from it—was by air.

Kai's morbid curiosity reached its peak. He didn't care about the risk anymore. It wasn't every day that you came face to face with a Collector. He might never have another chance.

The hovercraft let him out on a terrace, impossibly high in the air. One false move, and he would topple down to a certain death. But Kai's eyes were on the door.

What would the Collector look like? He was half imagining a monster, terrifying and not quite human.

But to his astonishment, the person who greeted him in the door was a small, old lady. She had white hair, a gentle face covered with fine wrinkles. She was leaning on a cane.

Kai forgot his tongue. This wasn't how he pictured a Collector at all. The lady reminded him more of Trish, his old employer back home—if Trish was wealthy, sweet-tempered, and very well preserved. That was the word that came to his mind. *Preserved.* The lady had to be at least a hundred years old.

"Young man." The old lady inclined her white head. "I believe you have something for me."

The two men stepped out of the hovercraft behind him. The shorter one carried the backpack. Behind them, the hovercraft pulled away from the edge of the terrace and dropped out of view.

Kai cleared his throat. "Yeah. It's a human arm," he said on impulse. There was a recklessness rising in him.

Behind him, the taller man made a low sound. A warning.

But the old lady only laughed, not perturbed in the slightest. "I certainly hope so." Then, turning back to the door, she gestured for Kai to follow her inside. "Please. Come in. It's not often I have visitors."

As Kai crossed the threshold, his skin prickled with unease. No matter how harmless his hostess looked, he was at her mercy now. He wouldn't be able to leave the loft unless she permitted it.

They stepped into a lavish foyer. There was a hallway on each side, and at the opposite end, a wide staircase split into two arms, which crossed and spiraled upward to the higher floors. Large, antique paintings in ornate frames hung on all the walls, and richly patterned rugs covered the tiled floor.

But the most impressive object was in the center of the room.

Real cut roses stood in a crystal vase on a round table.

They were blood red and so fragrant, they made Kai lightheaded for a moment. He had never seen a rose except in photos online. He couldn't imagine how much one cost.

The old lady gave a small wave of her hand, and the man with the backpack turned and hurried down the hallway. The taller man stood some distance away, motionless like a statue.

The old lady turned to Kai. "Will you have tea with me, Mr. Reed?"

Kai startled. She knew his name. His real name. *How?* He was speechless.

"Oh, of course I know who you are. But don't be concerned. You're quite safe here."

"You know my name. But I don't know yours." Kai blurted out. "Who are you?"

The old lady studied him for a moment. "Indeed, I imagine you don't follow politics." She raised her chin proudly. "My name is Dr. Olympia Livingstone. But let's sit down. Tea will be ready momentarily." She led him into a sitting room.

The room was decorated in the same lavish style as the foyer, and another dozen of blood-red roses stood in a blue vase on a low table.

Dr. Livingstone took a seat on a sofa and pointed to a sofa opposite hers. "Please, make yourself comfortable. Oh, and here's our tea."

A young woman had just brought in a tray with a teapot and two delicate cups. She poured the tea and withdrew without once lifting her gaze. Steam drifted up from the cups.

The tall bodyguard closed the door after her and

then resumed his post by the wall.

The old lady picked up her tea cup and peered at Kai's face. "So, Mr. Reed. You requested to see me. I daresay you have questions."

Kai took a deep breath. He did. Starting with this one... "*Why* do you collect them? The human body parts, I mean?"

"Ah. Straight to the point." Olympia Livingstone took a sip of her tea. "I'm afraid my answer won't satisfy you. But let me give it anyway. I collect them to safeguard the original designs, if you will. And to study them."

"*Study* them?"

"Oh yes. I'm a biologist by training. I taught at a university for many, many years." Her voice hardened. "Back when we still had scientific research aimed at building knowledge and understanding the natural world, rather than only at immediate and profitable applications." She gestured at Kai's untouched cup. "But your tea is getting cold. Please, drink."

Kai picked up his cup and drank, but he barely tasted the tea. He was too busy trying to fit together pieces of information that just didn't fit.

He had finally met a Collector, but she was nothing like what he had pictured. She was an old, gentle woman. She was a scientist. She had taught at a university. Except for her wealth, which made sense, everything about her surprised and confused him. More questions swarmed in his mind.

But before he could pick one, a side door opened, and a thin, white-haired man wearing a suit walked in. "Madam, I am sorry to interrupt. But the Council asks for your presence. We're ready to vote."

Olympia Livingstone straightened. "Very well." She put her cup back on the tray, picked up her cane, and rose to her feet. "You'll have to excuse me, Mr. Reed. I have a lot to do and not much time left to do it in." Then she added, "I know you have a lot of questions. I hope you'll find the answers you're looking for."

Kai got up. "Thanks."

She crossed to the adjacent room, an office.

Kai caught a glance of a large, executive desk and a dozen screens on the wall. A face peered from each screen, each of them stern and white-haired. Then the door closed, and the Collector was gone.

The tall man materialized next to Kai. He pointed to the main door. "We're going this way."

Kai handed the man his empty cup. "Thanks for the tea."

The hovercraft was already waiting for him outside.

It wasn't until his feet touched the ground again that a thought struck him.

If the Collector knew his real name, what else did she know? Did she know about Emily? Was that what she meant about him having a lot of questions?

But it was too late to ask.

13
EMILY

EMILY WAS BACK in the empty apartment. She sat on the sofa with her tablet in her lap. Her hands flew over the touchscreen, where the database shifted and merged endlessly.

"Oh, come on," she muttered, when another folder slipped from her reach. Her eyes burned, and her hands were starting to cramp. She had been at it for hours and had nothing to show for it.

Finally, she had had enough. She pushed the tablet off her lap, fighting the impulse to hurl it across the room. She had gotten one file—Sylvia's file—by sheer luck. But she needed the rest of them. People were going to die if she didn't figure out how to make the database stand still. And time was running out.

She got up from the sofa and crossed to the window. Wrapping her arms around herself, she turned her face to the glass.

Outside, the smog was rolling in, first blurring the outlines of buildings, then obliterating them from sight altogether. The highway was completely gone, nothing but a sea of gray in its place. It was like someone was erasing the city, block by block.

Emily let her gaze go unfocused as she contemplated the decision in front of her.

No matter how much she hated to admit it, she'd overestimated herself. She thought she could do it alone, but she couldn't. She needed help.

And there was only one man who could help her—even if Emily had vowed never to team up with him again. Never to speak to him again. But now she could see no way around it. This wasn't personal. Something much bigger was at stake.

Her decision made, there was no point in delaying the action. She picked up her tablet from the sofa and slipped it into her backpack, then grabbed her long coat.

She took one last look around the apartment. No matter how things went—well or very badly—she wouldn't return.

She walked out the door.

The apartment was in another sector, but she craved the exercise. She needed to clear her mind.

So she ran the whole distance, racing down one street after another. She pushed herself until her mind emptied of thoughts. Until there was only the rhythm of her own feet beating the asphalt and the sharp taste of the city air in her lungs.

But there was something else she was aware of, and the presence became stronger the longer and faster she ran. She was no longer alone. A ghost of another runner kept her company, whether she liked it or not.

The apartment building looked unchanged, as if only a day had passed instead of more than two years. She almost lost her nerve. But she couldn't walk away now.

She climbed to the seventh floor and stood in front of the familiar door. She knocked.

The door opened, and a tall young man appeared. One of his eyes was brown, the other blue. These strange eyes now took her in. "It's you."

Emily's heart swelled in her chest. He hadn't changed at all. "Hi, Xander. Can I come in?"

Xander held the door open for her, his eyes never

leaving her face. "It's your apartment too."

Emily took a step back. "Okay, listen. I'm here because I need your help. But that's all. That's the deal. Do you understand?"

"Whatever you want," he said. "I don't have much choice. Just... come in."

She hesitated, gripped by doubt. What was she doing here? This was wrong. She had promised herself she wouldn't do this. She should turn around and walk away right now.

But instead, she stepped inside, and Xander closed the door behind her.

The living room, which opened into the kitchen, was a mess. A large computer desk stood near the window, cluttered with electronics and old printed manuals. Clothes lay strewn all over the floor. The sofa looked like someone had been using it for a bed.

The only neat thing in the room was a clean, white wall, like a blank canvas waiting for a painter.

Emily glanced toward the short hallway and the bedroom at the end. She wanted to ask why he didn't sleep there. But she knew the reason.

The bedroom had been hers for the short time she had stayed here, when she had nowhere else to go and Xander took her in. He was three years older than her, and she was hopelessly in love with him then, while he treated her like a younger sister.

It wasn't until later that his feelings changed. But by then, he was a different person. And so was she.

"Sorry about that." Xander crossed to the sofa. He grabbed the cover he slept under, picked up some clothes from the floor, rolled them together, and threw them in the corner of the room. "I would've cleaned if I knew you were coming."

But Emily walked over to the computer desk instead. "I need your help with something." She shrugged off her backpack, pulled out her tablet, and loaded it into the docking station.

"Show me." Xander turned to the blank wall, his strange eyes bright with anticipation.

A moment later, a hologram of the database was projected in front of the wall. For a heartbeat, the complicated 3D structure stood still. Thousands of folders connected by a dense net of cross links, each with multiple levels of subfolders half-visible within in.

Then the database sprang into motion.

"Wow. Okay." Xander moved a step closer, as if drawn to the hologram by an invisible magnet. His eyes scanned the structure, which stretched, divided, merged, and turned inside out in ways that defied all rules of physics. He was completely absorbed, but his hands remained by his sides.

Emily watched him, and impatience burned in her.

She knew him. She knew what he was doing. He wanted to crack the problem, to see the pattern, before he ever looked at the code. It was the thrill of a challenge. Once he touched the code, the solution would be right there, and the fun would be over. The task was too easy to satisfy him.

Would this database be the same? Part of her ardently hoped so. The other part resented it.

"So what do you think?" she pressed. "Can you get to the code?"

Xander threw her a reproachful look. She was breaking the rules.

But he stepped closer, lifted his arms, and slipped his hands into the hologram. His fingers moved in rapid, well-practiced motions.

Emily held her breath.

There were ways to pull up the code, and even to edit it, right within the holo-environment. She had seen

Xander demonstrate the skill many times, although she had never mastered it herself.

But this time, Xander's skill wasn't enough. His fingers signed, traced, and grasped into the projection, but no code appeared. Neither did the database stop shifting, turning, and changing shape before their eyes.

Xander dropped his hands to his sides and turned to her, a mix of puzzlement and excitement on his face. "Did you see that? I can't get access!"

"But you have to!" Emily exclaimed. This wasn't a game. If Xander couldn't help her, she didn't know what else to do. An icy dread cut through her at the thought.

He must have read all this in her face, because his manner and expression turned serious. "This is important to you, isn't it?" He studied her. "Otherwise you wouldn't have come here."

Emily shivered. "Yes. It's very important to me."

Xander was only two feet away, his strange eyes still locked on hers. "Why?"

Her pulse quickened. She had forgotten how piercing his gaze could be.

There was a time when she cared about him more than anyone or anything in the world. He was as close to her as her own heartbeat, as necessary to her as the air she breathed. But that time had passed. She couldn't afford to feel that way about anyone anymore.

"It doesn't matter why," she said. "It's... none of your concern."

It was safer for both of them if he knew as little as possible. Besides, even if she told him everything, he wouldn't see it the way she did. Maybe the old Xander would have—the Xander she had fallen in love with. But not the new Xander. The new Xander was only helping her because she asked him. He had made his choice. She had no illusions about that.

"I see," he said. "So what do you need from me?"

"I need you to break it open so I can get the files," she said. "Can you do it?" It was a challenge. A dare.

"I think so. I've never failed yet," he said cautiously. "But it may take some time."

"I know." She tossed her head. "I saw you just now."

Xander smiled.

"What?" she snapped.

He shook his head. "Nothing. I just... like the new look. It suits you, Em."

She tensed. He meant the plastic surgery she had had after the accident, when she needed to disappear. A new face and a new identity. But it was the name that got to her. *Em.* Someone else had called her by that name not long ago, and she didn't want to be reminded.

"Thanks. But I go by Emily now."

If Xander heard the warning in her voice, he ignored it. "Why? What's wrong with Em?" He was still smiling, but there was an edge to his words. "Emma. Emily. *Em.* It still works." He paused. "Oh, right. I get it. It's what your Runner called you."

It hurt more than she expected, and the words rushed from her mouth. "And you would know. You listened to every word!" She had known about the audio recordings but wasn't planning to bring it up. Now it was too late.

Xander paled but kept her gaze. He didn't deny it. He didn't say anything. Maybe there was nothing to say.

She knew why he had done it, and she may have done the same thing in his place. But did that excuse him?

They looked at each other, the air suddenly thick with memories, good and bad.

"I tried to find you," Xander said, genuine pain in his voice.

Emily held his gaze. "I didn't want to be found."

Xander only studied her for a moment. Then he sighed. "You're after Falcon."

"Damn right, I'm after him!" All of a sudden, her control was gone, her heart pounding and the familiar fury choking her. "He has to pay for what he did!"

"I know you blame him for what happened to Ian." Xander spoke gently, cautiously. "But what if Falcon isn't so bad? What if we could do much worse than him?"

Ian.

Emily shuddered at the sound of the name, the fire in her veins instantly gone and her whole body turned to ice. "There's no one worse than Falcon."

They were both silent for a moment.

Then Xander cleared his throat. "Are you hungry? Let me make you something to eat."

"Okay." She was relieved to change the subject.

Xander crossed to the kitchen and busied himself with the food printer. "You can have your old bedroom," he said, not looking at her. "I prefer the sofa, anyway."

Emily's throat tightened, the memories crowding in. Xander taking her in and taking care of her when she had nowhere else to go. How could she ever pretend he was a stranger? They would always share a connection, no matter what happened, no matter how much both of them had changed.

She made her voice firm when she replied. "That would be good. Thanks."

But she was glad Xander couldn't see her face.

14
KAI

IT WAS NIGHTTIME, and Kai was walking down a dark street in the now-familiar sector, retracing his steps back to the house, back to Val, Leah, and the others. Apart from a few drones that had passed overhead, the last few blocks were deserted. He didn't see or hear a single person.

He had left behind the business district and the Training Center a good hour ago. But he wasn't in a rush, walking instead of running. A lot had happened today, and he was still processing it.

His thoughts kept circling back to the white-haired lady with her gentle face and her high-security loft; with her tea and her roses and her collection of human limbs in bio-support tanks, no doubt on display in one of the elegant rooms. The contrasts were puzzling and unsettling. He wished he had asked the Collector more questions when he had the chance.

Kai was so absorbed that he didn't notice the men until they stepped right in front of him.

There were two of them.

He slowed, instantly alert, ready to dodge them and break into a sprint—when a powerful blow to his lower back knocked the air out of him.

He gasped and wheeled around. Two more men were behind him. "What do you want?" His left side throbbed and he couldn't seem to pull in a full breath.

"Get him," one man said to the others. "The bastard is fast. We don't want him to get away."

Two men grabbed Kai by the arms and half walked, half dragged him into an alley.

Fast. So it wasn't a random attack. They knew him.

Kai made an effort to block the pain and focus. The men didn't wear masks, and they looked vaguely familiar.

"He's not going anywhere." The two men spun him around and slammed him against the wall.

Kai's back screamed with renewed pain, and he swayed on his feet, on the edge of blacking out. But he clenched his teeth and made no sound.

Because he knew them now, and he wouldn't give them the satisfaction.

It had been a year since he had run into them on the awe-inspiring, 3D-printed bridge inside the Training Center, but the scene was seared into his memory. It was the first day he used his wheelchair. The men stood tall and long-legged behind Slayer, cheering him on as he taunted Kai about his cut off feet. It was Kai's first encounter with Slayer as well.

Slayer. Kai hadn't thought of him in months. A mistake.

But now the attack made sense. It was just like Slayer to fight dirty—and with other men's fists instead of his own. Some things never changed.

Two men were still holding his arms to the wall. The other two drew closer. They all sneered at him. "You don't look so hot now, Sand Runner."

"No? I feel *great.*" The words just slipped out. Another mistake.

"Do you really?" A vicious blow to his stomach bent him in half. He would have crumbled to his knees if the other two men hadn't yanked him upright by his arms. "How about now?"

Kai muttered a curse, which only brought harsh laughter from the men. They sounded like hyenas, just like on the bridge that day. He seriously considered shaking them off, grabbing the nearest one, and smashing his head against the wall.

But it would be suicide, and something told him he might still make it.

They weren't here to kill him. The blows were calculated to inflict pain more than real damage. But then what *did* they want? Or, more to the point, what did Slayer want? Because there wasn't a doubt in Kai's mind that Slayer had sent them and given them precise instructions on what to do to him.

He knew he should keep his mouth shut, but he couldn't help himself. He never had patience for stupidity. "Slayer let you off the leash, huh?"

The men looked at one another. They clearly didn't expect to be recognized. Then one man drew closer, aiming a fist at Kai's nose. "You think you're so smart?"

But the other grabbed his wrist. "Not the face or the head, remember?"

Kai smiled inwardly. So he was right on both counts. They worked for Slayer, and he had given them specific instructions. He even spotted the familiar earrings. And they were stupid. Kai was right about that too.

"Alright. Let's finish this." One man reached inside his jacket. "I'm sick of him already."

Kai froze, expecting a gun or a knife. What if they *were* planning to kill him? His mind was racing, his muscles tense. He shifted his weight to one leg, ready to kick.

But the man produced a rolled tablet.

He unrolled it to its full size and turned it toward Kai.

A video call.

Slayer looked at him from the screen. He sat in an

executive chair, his arms behind his head and his prosthetic feet up on the desk. He wore a crisp white shirt with rolled-up sleeves. He looked pleased with himself, as if he'd had a productive day, and was now ready to relax.

"You look like shit," he said to Kai. "What happened to you?"

Kai ignored the mockery. The less he spoke, the better. "What do you want?"

"I'm afraid... I have bad news," Slayer said.

"What is it?" Kai's pulse sped up. He had assumed this was about him. Slayer sending thugs to beat him up. But what if he was wrong? What if Slayer did something worse?

On the screen, Slayer smiled an icy smile. He took his time to answer, rolling his chair from side to side as if he was bored. But he watched Kai the whole time.

Kai couldn't stand it anymore. "What bad news, Slayer?" he repeated. "Spit it out. Every psycho wants an audience." He bit his tongue too late.

The men in the alley shifted and exchanged glances, their eyes wide. He sensed something like respect from them. Although that wouldn't stop them from pummeling him to death if Slayer gave a sign.

But Slayer only looked amused. "A *psycho?* Indeed. If you mean high-functioning psychopathy, I did score at the top of the scale. Father was very concerned." His eyes got harder, and he leaned toward the camera and Kai. "But you miss one point. I'm not the actor here. I'm the audience. It's you who's been providing the entertainment." Then he added. "Well—you and your friends."

Your friends.

Images of Leah, Green, Val, and the others sprang to Kai's mind, and a raw, desperate anger surged through him. "You bastard!" He freed one of his arms and lunged forward to grab the tablet. "What did you to them? If you hurt them—"

Another mean punch to the ribs folded him in half and emptied his lungs of air. This time, he was allowed to drop to his knees.

Slayer looked down on him from the screen, unmoved. "Me? What did *I* do? Nothing, of course. I wasn't anywhere near the house when it happened. And... it's not over yet." That last part was a hiss of a snake.

Kai looked up. *Not over yet.* What did that mean?

He got to his feet, his breathing still ragged, but a fire pulsing through his veins. He glared at the screen. "This is between you and me. Leave them out of it. I'll race you any time."

"Race me?" Slayer's lips curled, and his eyes flashed, but his voice was cold and measured. "I don't want to race you. I want to crush you. I want to destroy you. I want to make you wish you were never born and you never had any friends."

This time, only Leah's face rose in Kai's mind, and a crippling fear stabbed his heart. He dropped his gaze. "Let me go," he pleaded.

"What was that? I couldn't hear you. Speak up." Slayer laughed.

Kai looked him in the eye. "Either kill me right now, or let me go!"

Slayer smiled. "Oh. Of course." He signaled to his men, and they stepped away from Kai. "Off you go then. *Run!* Before I change my mind."

For another heartbeat, Kai didn't move. He watched Slayer's face, letting every detail burn into his memory. If he ever needed anger or hate, it would be there, an infinite supply of it.

Then he turned and raced from the alley and down the street, in the direction of the house, dread fueling his steps.

15
KAI

KAI SPRINTED the rest of the way to the house, his lungs screaming and his ribcage still on fire from the blows Slayer's thugs had inflicted. Whole city blocks were steeped in darkness, without a single street light, and he tripped over the cracked ground, more distracted than ever.

What would he see when he got there? What had Slayer done?

By the time he turned onto their street, he was frantic. He imagined he heard screams and smelled smoke from a fire.

But the night was silent, the air unusually clear.

The house itself looked peaceful and unchanged, the peeling walls still standing, the window on the ground floor coated with smog, but intact. For a moment, hope flared in Kai's chest. Maybe Slayer was just torturing him. Maybe Leah and the others were all safely asleep inside.

But when he tried the front door, it swung open at his touch. It hadn't been closed properly. The lock rattled in the frame, broken and useless.

It wasn't over yet, Slayer had told him.

Kai stepped inside, all senses on high alert.

He paused in the dark foyer, listening. But all he heard was his own racing heartbeat.

The house was quiet. Too quiet.

Where was everyone? Kai had an impulse to yell out

for them but stopped himself.

He glanced around and recoiled.

A human shape lay in the shadow near the wall.

Kai hurried over, dreading who it might be.

But it wasn't a person. The ancient electric fan had been smashed to pieces, the drum bent and the large wooden blades snapped off.

Bending over it, Kai examined a thick, wide blade where it had been broken off. It was a clean cut, the edge smooth, without splinters. No hand or foot could have done it. Not even a knife. Whoever did it used an ax.

Kai imagined Slayer's thugs wielding axes and shuddered at the thought.

Where was Leah? Did the attackers come when she and Ana were alone in the house?

Weak light came from the kitchen, and Kai started down the hallway toward it.

On passing an open door, plastic crunched under his feet. He scanned the workroom.

It looked like a hurricane had blown through it—shelves torn from the walls and the table upended. Piles of parts and circuit boards lay scattered on the floor, together with the bins and the tools.

The tools.

Kai stopped short. The tools were valuable. No robber would leave them behind. So Slayer's men didn't break into the house to pilfer. They had another agenda. But what?

As if in answer, a muffled cry came from the kitchen.

Leah.

Abandoning all caution, Kai ran down the hallway and into the kitchen.

He caught a glimpse of someone tied to a chair—limp arms, head drooping, shirt covered with blood—and a heavy ax on the floor.

"Kai—*stop!*"

He stopped a second before running into a blade aimed at his throat.

He turned and met a fierce gaze.

Ana stepped away from him, lowering her knife. "I'd be more careful if I were you." A nasty bruise bloomed on her cheekbone.

Leah rushed toward him. She was the one who had warned him. She threw Ana a reproachful look. "Kai! I thought you weren't coming back." She touched his side, and he flinched. "You're hurt."

"I'm fine. But how are you?" He was relieved to see her, but worry still gnawed at him. He peered into her face. What had happened here?

Leah looked pale and tired, with dark circles under eyes. But she gave him a weak smile. "We're alright. But... oh, Kai... It was terrible." Tears welled up in her eyes.

Without a word, Ana crossed the room and swung a hard kick at the chair. The person tied to it twitched and moaned, as if waking from a nightmare.

Kai turned to see the prisoner—and shock rolled over him.

It was a boy, no older than twelve. With dirty hair and a bloodied lip. The ax on the floor next to the chair looked too heavy for him to pick up.

What sick game was Slayer playing?

"Who is this?" Kai asked.

"Someone who's going to regret ever walking into this house." Ana flicked her knife. She swung another kick at the chair, and the boy shuddered and whimpered. "He's already regretting it now."

Kai frowned at her. "What are you doing? He's not even awake."

"Of course not. I drugged him. But he can feel fear, so that's what I'm giving him. He doesn't deserve a nice dream." She flicked her knife and swung her leg for another kick.

But Leah caught her arm. "Stop it. Just... please." She sounded out of breath.

Ana's expression softened. The knife stilled in her hand. It was like Leah's touch drained the anger from her. "Fine. I'll stop. Let Val decide what to do with them."

"Them?" Kai asked.

But just then, Green rushed in, his glasses sliding down his nose. "What is it? Are they back? I heard something!"

Ana stepped toward him, the blade again restless in her fingers. "You're asking *me* if they're back. Really? You were supposed to guard the front door."

"Sorry." Green nervously fiddled with his glasses. "I just had to... check something upstairs really quick."

Ana scowled. "Let me guess. The stupid Boards?"

Green paled. "They're not stupid."

"Oh, wake up, Green. Nobody's out there. Nobody cares." She wiped the knife on her pant leg and slipped it into her boot. "You either learn to fend for yourself, or you die. Simple as that."

"Where's Val?" Kai cut in. "And the others?"

Green turned, only now noticing him. "Kai! Oh. They're not back yet. But they should be here soon."

"Not back yet?" How could that be? Val headed home hours ago, and he knew all the shortcuts.

"They got back from the job an hour ago," Ana explained. "Now they're tracking down his buddies." She pointed to the boy tied to the chair. "So we can all have a little talk."

Kai's body turned cold. He had seen glimpses of Val's hot temper. Was that Slayer's plan? To provoke Val's rage and then watch him unleash it on a bunch of kids? Was that the entertainment he had in mind? It suited him, the sick bastard.

"Come on. Why not just let him go? What's the big deal?" Kai tried to sound off-hand. "What did he do? Break the fan and make a mess in the workroom? He's just a kid."

"'What's the big deal?'" Ana spun toward him, eyes flashing. "Go see the greenhouse! See if you still want to let him go then!"

The greenhouse.

Kai's chest tightened, and his eyes shot to Leah.

But her gaze was down, her lips trembling.

He turned and ran up the dark stairs, taking two, then three steps at a time. Smashed lightbulbs littered the steps. The shattered glass turned to powder under Kai's prosthetic feet.

On the second-floor landing, a single light flickered, illuminating a deep gash in the wall.

The ax again.

Anger stirred in Kai's gut. Stealing was one thing. Pointless destruction was another.

The greenhouse was a heartbreaking sight.

The lights had been spared here, as if to ensure that, day or night, the destruction could be beheld in all its painful detail.

In every direction, small trees and bushes lay chopped down, vines had been ripped off the poles that had supported them, roots torn out of the dirt and stomped to a shapeless mass.

Kai walked down the narrow path, searching for a patch that had escaped the wrath. But he found none. Whoever did this went out of their way not to leave a plant untouched.

And it couldn't have been just one person, either. A group of people did this. And it took work—it took effort.

Kai came to the corner where Leah had fixed the switch for an irrigation line. Someone's boot had systematically smashed the pipes and torn the wires every few steps. No plants would be watered by this irrigation line again. It would have to be rebuilt from scratch.

Kai stopped, his heart pounding and his teeth clenched. It was painful to see so much loving labor turned to ruin. But worst of all, the violence was senseless, the destruction stupid. Why smash something if you can steal it and eat it, or grow it and enjoy it for years to come?

His own words echoed in his head. Why not just let him go? What's the big deal?

He shook his head now. *No.* Ana was right. It *was* a big deal. No one was just walking away from this.

"Kai! Come on!" Green urged him from the door. "They're here. We're going to have a trial!"

A trial.

The word shocked Kai into clarity.

The sectors had no police force and no courts of law. The security drones were only there to protect the rich. People dealt with crime on their own.

"Green, wait! I have to talk to you."

Reluctantly, Green let the door close behind him. "Okay. What is it? They're about to start. We should head down."

Kai searched for the right words, but none came, so he simply said. "It's my fault this happened."

Green's eyes blinked once behind his thick lenses. "What do you mean? How can it be your fault?"

"These kids didn't just decide to do this on their own. Someone told them to do it—probably paid them too."

"Paid them? What for?" Green shook his head in confusion. "And how is that your fault?"

"It's my fault because... that person wanted to hurt *me*," Kai said.

"How do you know?"

"He told me so." Kai gritted his teeth. "After the fact, of course. So I couldn't do anything to stop it." A bitter anger choked him.

Green looked thoughtful. "That doesn't make it your fault. You didn't do anything. And..." He hesitated. "I don't think you should tell anyone else about it." He glanced toward the door.

"Why not?"

Green spoke firmly. "Because it won't solve anything if you do. And... I don't think Val would let you stay."

It was like a punch to the stomach.

Green was right. Val wouldn't take any chances. Not where the group's safety was concerned. After all, who was Kai to them? He was still a stranger. What did he contribute to the group, to ask them to take this risk in return? Not nearly enough.

"Thanks, Green. I appreciate it." He had made one friend at least.

"No problem. Now we really have to go. Come on." And Green hurried out the door.

With a heavy heart, Kai followed.

A murmur of agitated voices and shuffling feet came from the kitchen. Kai got to the door and scanned the scene.

On one side, Ana and Zip towered over a bunch of skinny kids in dirty clothes, who stood huddled together, terror in their eyes.

Karim and Hans were just lifting the chair with the boy still tied to it. They carried it to the table and started untying the kid's arm.

Behind them stood Marco, clutching a first-aid kit.

And by the table, erect and stone-faced, stood Val. Holding the ax.

Kai stared at the scene in front of him as if from miles away, not comprehending.

Leah rushed to her brother's side. "No, Val! You can't

do this! It's *wrong!"*

"The majority decided, Leah." Val glanced at the others, and they somberly nodded. "We're not rich. These punks broke into our home and destroyed our work and our property for no good reason. They tried to hurt you and Ana! They have to be punished."

Val glanced at Ana, and she crossed the room and took Leah's arm, restraining her.

Leah tried to shake her off. "Let go of me! This never would have happened if you'd let me talk to them instead of getting me out of the way!"

But already, Karim was lifting the drugged boy's arm onto the table.

Val gripped the ax more tightly. "Hold him." His voice rang with finality.

In desperation, Leah freed her arm from Ana's grip and rushed between her brother and the boy. She was shaking all over, her breathing shallow and her cheeks and eyes feverish with urgency. "*No.* I won't allow it. I don't care what he did. He doesn't deserve this." She extended her pale wrist. "Cut off my hand instead."

Kai leapt forward. "*Stop!"* he cried. "She's right! The kids aren't responsible."

He had expected an outburst of anger, but Val only looked exasperated. "Then who is? *Who* is responsible?"

Kai took a deep breath. "I am."

16
KAI

SILENCE FILLED the kitchen after Kai had spoken, thick and airless as smog. All eyes turned on him. Even the kids stared, the terror in their faces turning into confusion and hope.

"*I'm* responsible," he repeated.

"How's that?" Val demanded. "You weren't even here."

Val's fire was gone. But his jaw was still set, and the ax remained in his hand.

Kai had to convince him. If he convinced the leader, he'd convince the whole group.

"Like you said, they broke into the house, but they didn't steal anything. They only destroyed stuff. Why? It doesn't make sense." Kai pointed to the boys. "Look at them. They're poor as dirt. They could have taken the tools from the workroom and gotten good money for them. And how about the plants? Real food! Anybody could see the plants were valuable."

"That just shows they're dumb," Ana scowled. "Tell us something we don't know."

"We're not dumb," a wiry boy piped up. One of his front teeth was missing.

The other kids murmured and nodded in agreement. Their courage was returning.

"Shut up, you little rat," Ana said.

But Kai turned to the kid. "I know you're not dumb.

It's tough out there on the streets. But you know how to survive. You can take care of yourself and your friends. You understand about jobs and money."

The boy lifted his chin. "Sure, I understand about jobs and money. And the name's Max."

Val had been listening patiently. But now he stepped in front of Kai. "Hold on! You're saying someone *hired* them to do this?"

The anxious looks on the boys' faces were proof enough. "We're not telling you nothing," Max said. But he, too, looked uneasy.

"That's exactly what I'm saying." Kai faced Val. "Someone told them what to do and paid them to do it."

"And who was that?" There was a warning in Val's voice.

"An enemy of mine." Kai pictured the cruel face, and anger flared in his chest. "Someone who's hated my guts for a while and found an opportunity to hurt me."

A look of understanding registered on Val's face, and he opened his mouth to speak. But then changed his mind.

"Hurt *you?"* Ana spit out. "How did they hurt *you* exactly? Did they jump you in your own house? Did they put an ax through your walls and cut up your stuff? Am I missing something here?" She turned to the group, looking from one person to another. "Because it looks to me like it was *us* who got hurt, and *he*," this with a sharp look at Kai, "got off scot-free."

Kai was silent. What could he say? That Slayer could have easily hurt him—but he chose to hurt his friends instead, because he knew it would bother Kai a whole lot more?

Leah crossed to Kai and lightly touched his arm. "We get it." She glanced at Ana. "We all have people we care about."

Ana's face changed, and she looked away.

For some reason, Leah's sympathy only made Kai feel worse. "No. Ana is right. I didn't get hurt. You guys did." He looked at Val, at Leah, at all of them. "But it's my fault this happened. I brought it on you."

As if on cue, the boy tied to the chair stirred and lifted his head, blinking. He tried to raise his hand, probably to push the stringy hair out of his eyes, but Karim caught his wrist. The boy's eyes popped open.

"What? What?" He took in the ropes that bound him, then the table, then the ax in Val's hand. He froze, his eyes huge with fear. "I had a nightmare. I think I'm still not woke."

Val sighed and put down the ax. "Untie him."

Relief lit up Leah's face. She gently pushed Karim aside and helped the boy herself. But the group exchanged confused looks.

Marco put away the first-aid kit, looking relieved. "So... now what?" he asked.

Val locked eyes with Max. "Now *the Rats* can pay us back for the damage and get out of here." He extended his hand. "Come on. You got paid something, didn't you? Let's see it. *All* of it."

Max hesitated. Then reached inside his shirt and pulled out a flat pouch.

Ana snatched it off his neck. She unzipped it, fished out the crumpled notes, and flipped through them. "That's it? Are you kidding me? It's not enough to fix the lock on the front door."

Max's face turned red. "We were going to get the rest *after*," he mumbled. "But not if we got caught." He was more ashamed of making a bad business deal than of all the meanness he committed.

"Then you'll stay here until you *work* it off," Leah declared. She glanced at her brother, as if expecting him to interrupt, and quickly added, "You can start with the workroom. Put it back the way it was, all the parts off the floor and properly sorted."

"Yeah!" Riko and Hans nodded, in favor of the idea.

Part of Kai was grateful for the distraction, but the other part wished the group would finish with him first, so he knew where he stood.

"You think you can handle the job?" Leah asked Max.

Max narrowed his eyes. "Who said we want to work for you?"

Ana pocketed the cash and tossed the empty pouch to the boy. "You owe us. Big time."

Max caught the pouch and pouted. "You can't force us."

Green had been quiet this whole time, but now he stepped forward. "No. But we can post on the Boards about you. The whole story. With all your mugshots. How would you like that?"

The mention of the Boards made an impression. Max paled. "You don't have to do that. We'll help out." He looked at his buddies, as if confirming the choice of strategy. "We're... sorry."

Everyone looked to Val for the final decision.

But the red-haired man wasn't looking at any of them. He stared into the air, his body tense and a deep frown on his face, as if he was inwardly wrestling with some tough question.

"Val?" Leah prompted.

Her brother roused himself. "We need to decide as a group..."

"I'll watch them," Leah offered. "They won't cause any more trouble."

But Val's eyes stopped on Kai. "...what to do about *him.*"

A hush fell over the kitchen as everyone turned to look at Kai.

Kai's heart pounded in his chest. This was it. They would judge him, and he would have no choice but to accept whatever they decided. It was only fair. "I understand."

"You can wait in Green's room," Val told him.

Green's face was pained. "Shouldn't we hear him out first?"

But Val had already turned to Ana, "Take the Rats to the spare bedroom. Zip, help her."

Ana gave a short nod, and she and Zip ushered Max and the others out of the kitchen.

Leah turned to her brother. "Green's right. We should—"

But Kai cut her off. "It's fine. I'll be in Green's room." He nodded to Val and walked out of the kitchen.

*

Green had always made Kai feel welcome. But now his cramped, cluttered quarters held no comfort.

Kai sat down with his back against the wall. The room was cold, and the chill seeped into his bruised ribs, into his tired muscles. His eyes wandered over the beat-up books and odd knickknacks filling the shelves, but his mind was elsewhere.

What would happen? What would the group decide? All he could do was wait.

He closed his eyes. The events of the last few hours replayed in his mind, the images passing through it one by one. Leah. Val. Ana. Max. The gash in the wall. The trashed greenhouse. The thugs in the alley.

And one memory, more urgent and intense than all the others.

Slayer's hateful face.

Kai's jaw clenched. Slayer was out of his reach for

now. But he would *not* get away with this. Kai had to think of something, had to find a way. And most of all, he had to make sure Slayer would never be able to hurt the people he cared about again.

Finally, exhaustion took over, and Kai slumped against the side of the bed, his head resting on his arm. Just before he fell into a dreamless slumber, one more image visited him, as comforting as it was painful.

Emily.

He hadn't given up on her, even if she had given up on him.

You hurt me the most. Do you know that? Do you care?

There was no answer.

17
EMILY

EMILY SAT UP in bed, her heart pounding.

She had had a strange dream. In it, she was running down one abandoned street after another, chasing a man she knew and missed, trying to catch up to him as he sprinted away a block ahead of her, trying to get him to stop and face her. But smog was drifting into the streets, erasing everything in its path, until she lost sight of him altogether.

She slowed at an intersection, looking helplessly at the graying streets that radiated out all around her, unsure which one to follow. Then she heard running footsteps behind her. Someone was chasing *her*, getting closer. Urgency filled her. She had to get away. Quick. But which way to go?

She woke up before she could decide.

Her dreaming mind got it wrong, anyway. She wasn't chasing Kai. If anything, she was hiding from him. But maybe the meaning was different. Kai was probably searching for her, wondering why she had left, maybe even doubting if she had ever been truthful with him. Or he might already hate her, as the man who called himself her Mentor in the Race had predicted, even if he had lied about everything else...

Emily pushed the thoughts away. There was nothing she could do right now. She had chosen a path she had to walk alone.

Faint light flickered in the hallway. Xander was still up. Emily got out of the bed and walked barefoot to the living room.

The hologram was up, and Xander stood with his hands immersed in the virtual structure, studying it intently.

Hope swelled in Emily's chest. The structure was motionless, and then it slowly moved to the right, obeying Xander's commands. Had he cracked the code behind the endless and maddening transformations while she was asleep?

But when she moved closer and got a better view, her hope turned to apprehension. The hologram didn't show the database. A close-up of a complicated electronic circuit hovered in the air.

Then Xander zoomed out, and the outer shape of the structure became visible, semi-transparent to show the familiar compartments, valves, and pipes.

It was a 3D model of an artificial heart.

And not just any heart. The product name, *Titan SI 200*, was hard to miss.

"What are you doing?" She rushed over.

Xander turned to her. "You're up. I just found it. I was going to show it to you in the morning."

"I already know what it is," Emily said. "But you have no business snooping around the database behind my back! I don't need your help searching it. Just make it stand still, and I'll search it myself."

Impatience flashed in Xander's eyes. "Em, if you know what it is, then what are you doing with it? I don't know how you got it. But you'll never be able to sell it."

"Sell it?" Emily cut in. "Who said anything about selling it?"

"Then whatever you're planning. An auction. Moving it part by part. Doesn't matter what it is. I can already tell you. It's *too* dangerous. No money is worth it."

"*Money?*" Emily's throat was tight. "Is that all you think about?"

"Don't be naïve," Xander said. "Even if *you* don't care about the money, that's what the file means to everybody else. The model puts 3D Electronics eons ahead of the competition. It contains a dozen innovations that will disrupt the market completely." He pointed at the hologram. "The information inside this file is *priceless.*" He shook his head. "Em, whatever you were planning, *forget* it. It'll never work. You need a *new* plan. And you need to be smart about it."

Emily stared at him hard. "So what? You're going to help me figure out this new plan, and then we split the money fifty-fifty?" She couldn't keep the bitterness out of her voice. It all came flooding back. The pain of watching someone she loved change into a near stranger. "Is that what's going to happen?"

A shadow passed over Xander's face. "Actually, I don't need the money. I make enough of it. I'm just looking out for you."

"Well—don't! I can look after myself." Guilt tugged at her. She had gone too far, but it was too late to take it back. "And the file isn't for sale, anyway. Nothing in the database is."

"So you were just testing me? Believe it or not, money isn't the only thing I care about." Xander watched her. "But you're right on one count. I'm *not* like you. I'm not trying to save the world."

"I'm not trying to save the world either." Embarrassment warmed her cheeks. "Just to set things right."

Xander smiled. He was still watching her. "Isn't that the same thing?"

"Listen. I want to look at this file now." She didn't have to explain herself to anybody, especially not to

Xander. "Can I do that?"

Xander stepped away from the hologram. "Sure. Go ahead." He grabbed his tablet and stretched on the sofa, his back to her.

He was giving her privacy. Or as much privacy as was possible in this cramped apartment.

Emily watched the back of his head for a moment longer.

Xander made most of his money as a swapper online, hacking into medical databases to help clients who wanted to make sure their new identity linked to the right DNA, in case anyone checked. It was a lucrative job, and he was rich by most standards. He could afford a much bigger apartment in a much better sector, even in the business district if he wished. And yet, Xander had chosen to stay in his old place, cramped as it was. Why?

She turned her attention to the hologram. With cautious motions, she examined the mechanical parts of the model and ran through simulations of their functions. She zoomed in and out on the arrays of electronics scattered throughout the heart.

To her non-expert eye, the design looked flawless. But she knew there was a flaw in it. There *had* to be.

Worse, the flaw had been deliberately added, and it served a specific and cruel purpose.

She had seen it in action.

As long as the patient paid the lease on time, the heart worked perfectly. But if the payment was missed, the device started to malfunction. First came the warnings. The patient experienced heartburn, dizziness, and shortness of breath. Nothing too severe but unpleasant enough they couldn't be ignored. But if the grace period ended and the lease was still not paid, the gloves were off. The device would simulate increasingly painful and life-threatening heart conditions—ending in death from cardiac arrest.

Sylvia's face rose to Emily's mind, and her own heart ached.

Sylvia had known what was coming. She had known she was going to die, even though her death was easy to prevent. *Money.* If she only had enough money to pay the lease, and to keep paying it each month, her artificial heart would keep on beating for two hundred years. But she had no money and no way to get it. Losing her job was a death sentence.

What was it like for Sylvia to know this? How could she bear it? Was there a worse, more crushing kind of helplessness than to know death was coming, and although there was a cure, an escape, this escape was forever out of reach?

Emily forced her attention back to the diagram. She examined it doggedly. But it was no use. The flaw could be glaring at her, and she would be clueless. She didn't understand the complicated electronic circuits. She had no idea what to look for.

But she knew someone who would.

Emily pulled her tablet out of the docking station. Back in the bedroom, she slipped the tablet into her backpack and quickly got dressed. Her long coat on, she grabbed the backpack and headed back to the living room.

Xander stood, waiting for her.

"I have to go," Emily said.

Color drained from his face, and he rushed toward her, catching her arm. "What? No. Wait—"

"I meant, I'm going out." Emily gently shook off his hand. "I'll be back."

"Then I'm coming with you." He grabbed his jacket and was back at her side. His strange eyes locked on her face.

"No. You can't. I'll be fine." Emily's voice was firm,

but her heart hammered in her chest. Xander's strange gaze had always unnerved her, and now there was a new intensity in it. But was it longing or greed?

"At least tell me where you're going," he said.

Emily looked away.

The less Xander knew, the better. She could never trust the new Xander the way she'd trusted the old one. But lying wouldn't work either. He could probably track her every step through the cameras of the city drones. So she told him the truth.

"I'm going to see Neen."

*

Emily got to Neen's lab at the break of dawn.

Andy opened the door. He didn't look happy to see her, and she didn't blame him. "What do you want?"

"I need to talk to Neen."

"I know someone else you need to talk to," he said darkly. "Maybe you should take care of that first." He still didn't invite her inside.

"Please, Andy. It's important." She hoped he wouldn't ask what it was about. She couldn't risk telling him. Andy had worked for Falcon once.

"Emily?" Neen peered at her from behind the Technician's broad back.

"Hi, Neen." Emily was relieved to see the Print Maker. She shrugged off her backpack and held it in front of her.

"Why are you standing in the door? Come in." Neen threw Andy a confused look.

He stepped aside, letting Emily enter. Then he turned and marched down the hallway toward the lab.

"He's upset about Kai," Neen told Emily.

Emily's heart gave a painful pang. "Why? What's

wrong? Is he hurt?"

Neen shook her head. "No, he's fine now. But we haven't heard from him for weeks. Andy's worried." Her eyes went to the backpack in Emily's hands. "But why are you here? We haven't seen you in even longer."

Emily took a deep breath. "I want to show you something... and ask for a favor." She pulled out her tablet and glanced toward the closest lab. "Could I use your docking station?"

Neen's eyes lit up when the hologram of the artificial heart appeared in front of her. "The new Titan."

"So you know it?" Hope kindled in Emily's chest.

"I've heard about it. Sure. But I've never seen the designs." Neen reached into the hologram and rotated the heart, examining it from all sides. "How did you get them?"

"Never mind that. I'll tell you another time," Emily said. "But right now I need your help."

Neen had switched the view to a detailed technical diagram and was studying it intently. "My help with what?"

"Finding the flaw."

Neen turned to look at her. "The *flaw?* Titan SI 200 has a flaw?" She sounded skeptical.

Emily had a sudden inspiration. "Maybe not a flaw. More like... a feature. An *off-switch*—something that causes the heart to malfunction in specific ways at specific times."

Neen faced the hologram again, scrolling through the 3D circuitry. "An off-switch?"

"Yes. Can you find it?"

Neen studied the circuits intently, already engrossed in the task. "I don't know. But I can try."

"Okay. I'll wait." Emily withdrew to the back of the room and settled down to watch. If there was an off-switch, Neen would find it. She just had to be patient.

But when Neen stepped away from the hologram a few hours later, she declared, "There is no off-switch. There is no flaw. The design is *perfect!"* She was ecstatic about the result.

Disappointment welled up in Emily like icy water, numbing her from inside. "I see." Her throat tightened around the words.

What now? She understood even less than before she had come here.

And she was running out of time.

18
KAI

A SHARP CREAK of the door hinges yanked Kai out of sleep. He sat up, blinking. He had fallen asleep on the floor.

Val stood in the door, his silhouette outlined by daylight. "You awake? I have to talk to you."

Kai got to his feet. "Yeah, I'm awake." He glanced around the room. "Where's Green?"

Val ignored the question and pulled the door closed.

He just stood there for a moment, looking at the wall, his expression grim. Then he turned to Kai. "I've got to say, I respect your honesty. The Rats would have probably given it away at some point. But you saved me a lot of second-guessing."

"Right." Thoughts rattled in Kai's mind. He was done here. Where to now? He could stop by to see Neen and Andy. Get his prostheses checked. But then what?

"You've got to understand, these people are my family." Val's tone was matter-of-fact. "I'm responsible for them. And I will not let anyone bring this kind of danger on them again."

"I do understand." Neen and Andy's lab. Then... nothing.

Suddenly, Val's calm was gone. "It was that Slayer guy, wasn't it?" He read the answer in Kai's face. "I thought so. You can tell he's a hater, and you beat him in the Race."

"He won't get away with it," Kai said.

"I don't know about that," Val said darkly. "But if he ever tries again, we'll be ready for him." He looked Kai straight in the eye. "And from now on, if anything is up, *you* come to *me*, and we decide how to handle it together. You got that?"

Kai blanched. "What? So... you don't want me to leave?"

"The group voted for you to stay," Val said. "The vote was unanimous."

Kai didn't know what to say. He didn't expect this kind of support. He wasn't sure he deserved it. "Thanks. I appreciate it."

"Don't thank *me*. I withheld my vote."

Strangely, that made Kai feel better. "Fair enough."

"Okay then. Get some breakfast. Then report to Zip. We've got a lot of work to do." Val pushed the door open and walked out of the room ahead of Kai.

*

Val was right about the work. Between the repairs and the clean-up, they all worked non-stop for days. The house was buzzing with activity.

Kai was grateful for something to do. It took his mind off of things he could do nothing about at the moment. Finding Emily. Making Slayer pay for what he did. Both of these would have to wait.

Zip had made a list of damages and assigned people to tackle each one. This included the kids, whom everyone called Rats now, thanks to Ana. Their first job was to put the workroom in order, and they accomplished it in a day without a complaint. After that, they helped out wherever help was needed, moving freely about the house.

Leah still kept an eye on them, but Kai suspected it was more to protect them than anything else. That was just Leah. There wasn't a vengeful bone in her body.

Max impressed everyone by fixing the lock on the front door, which he had also picked in the first place. Axer, nicknamed after the weapon he brought into the house, tried to rebuild the electric fan he had smashed but had to give up. Another boy turned out to be a girl in disguise, Max's sister, Brie, and she quickly attached herself to Leah, following her like a shadow.

Everyone threw themselves into the work. Even the Rats gave it all they had. If anything, Val had to remind people to eat and rest and not too push themselves too hard. But they didn't listen.

Soon enough, the house was in working order again. Although some signs of the attack remained, like the gash in the wall, patched up but still visible.

It reminded Kai of the man on the elevator in the Training Center, with a scar across his neck where someone had tried to slit his throat. The Mentor, as he introduced himself to Kai later on, when he tried to take Emily's place as his Agent on the last day of the Race. As if Kai would ever let that happen.

The work on the repairs was rewarding enough. But now Kai had something else to lift his spirits. They had all voted for him to stay. The whole group. Well—everyone except Val. But it was still a relief. It meant he didn't have to wonder anymore if they wanted him out. He may not be close friends with everyone—Ana definitely held no warm feelings for him—but he was part of the group. And that was enough.

It also made him homesick. He wondered about Ron and Sam and the others. How were they doing? He hadn't talked to them in ages. But if he called them, they were sure to ask about Emily. And then what? He couldn't lie to them and pretend everything was fine when Emily was gone, and he still had no idea why.

No, he couldn't call Ron or Sam right now. Not yet. Not until he knew what had happened.

With the most urgent repairs to the rest of the house done and out of the way, Kai now spent most of his time working in the greenhouse alongside Leah, Ana, and the others.

The greenhouse had suffered the most damage, both to the plant life and to the support systems, and their progress in restoring it to its former state was painfully slow.

Fortunately, not all the plants were destroyed as Kai had thought. Leah's sharp eye and gentle fingers found precious survivors under the chopped and smashed plant carcasses, and those were lovingly replanted in the corner of the greenhouse that had been cleaned and readied for that purpose. Leah carried out these difficult and delicate rescue operations entirely by herself, while also directing six or seven helpers in multiple other tasks, from clean-up to rebuilding the irrigation system. Still, the greenhouse continued to be a heartbreaking sight.

Not surprisingly, the work took a toll on her. Always pale, Leah's skin now had a blueish tone. After kneeling at her task, she would get up slowly, as if unsure of her balance, and use the wall for support as she walked.

Once she swayed on her feet and nearly fell. Kai rushed toward her, but Ana was closer and got there first, catching her friend's arm. "*Leah!*"

But Leah pushed Ana's hands away. "I'm fine. Stop fussing."

Kai watched them, puzzled and uneasy. Something had changed between Leah and Ana since the attack. What did Leah say to her after Val brought the Rats back for the trial? Something about Leah wanting to talk to the kids when they broke into the house and Ana not letting her. Although that couldn't be right. How could Leah talk to an attacker swinging an ax?

Ana caught him looking and glared at him.

Then she turned and marched to the door. Axer scuttled out of her way.

While the others treated the Rats with differing degrees of friendliness, Ana still barely tolerated them. And Kai didn't blame her. The bruise on her cheekbone was still there, slow to heal.

"What exactly happened during the attack?" Kai asked Green later that day. "Do you know?"

Green was busy working on his computer, like he was most days. He helped with the clean-up and repairs, same as everyone, but he always hurried up to his room any time he wasn't needed, even if it was for just a few minutes. But whatever he was working on, Kai got a sense Green wasn't ready to talk about it.

So he asked about the attack instead. It didn't take much encouragement for Green to turn away from his computer and spill the story.

"Oh, man." He shook his head in awe. "But I have to tell it from the beginning."

It turned out Ana's parents had been pharmacists and worked in research. She grew up around drugs and learned how they worked and how to use them. "I don't mean she took drugs herself." Green fidgeted in his chair. "I mean she learned how to use them on other people. Like... a doctor."

"Right. She drugged Axer," Kai cut in. "But what about Leah? Why is Leah mad at her?"

Green looked uneasy. "Ana drugged her too."

"What! *Why?*"

"She had no choice. Leah wouldn't listen. She just refused."

Kai stared at him. "What are you talking about? Refused to do what? Just... slow down."

"Okay. Sorry," Green said. "Ana heard the attackers first and tried to get Leah to the safe room—"

"We have a safe room?" Kai cut in again. "I didn't know that."

Green gave him a look. "It wouldn't be very safe if everyone knew about it. Anyway, that's our emergency procedure. That's what we're supposed to do if someone breaks in and there are only a few of us here. Val's orders. Our lives are more important than any stuff we own."

"So Ana drugged Leah to get her into the safe room?" Kai was still processing the information.

"Yeah. I don't know what she used. But it was something safe and quick. Ana is always prepared, ever since..." Green stopped himself. "Anyway. Leah is mad for two reasons. One, she saw the guys who broke in were just kids, and she wanted to talk to them, but Ana wouldn't hear of it. And two, Ana was supposed to get in the safe room herself—"

"But she didn't," Kai said.

"Nope. She locked Leah in and then fought with the kids on her own."

"Red sands," Kai muttered. "That was pretty brave of her." He had to admire Ana's guts. And her devotion to Leah.

"For sure," Green agreed. "But Val isn't happy with her either. She put her life at risk."

"But she meant well." Kai felt a sudden sympathy for Ana. "And it's her house. Her family lived here. She couldn't just let someone trash it."

"I guess." Green sighed. "Too bad she didn't stop them from trashing the greenhouse."

Kai thought of Leah's pale face, of her slender fingers coaxing a fragile sapling back to life, and his chest tightened. "I know. But... we'll get it back. We'll rebuild it. It'll just take time."

Green turned back to his computer. "Right. Sure." But his voice sounded hollow.

*

Still, the greenhouse looked a little greener and a little healthier each day. First one patch of plants returned, then another. Then a whole row was back.

But as the greenhouse got better, Leah got worse. She was pushing herself too hard, insisting on doing more than anyone else. And worst of all, refusing help.

Finally, Kai couldn't stand it in anymore.

Leah had risen from a patch of herbs she'd been working on and now stood with her palm flat against the wall, swaying lightly.

Kai walked up to her and touched her arm. "You okay?"

She turned to him, her cheeks a feverish pink. "Kai." She smiled. "I'm fine." She took a step—and fainted.

"Whoa!" Kai caught her, one arm behind her shoulders, the other closing around her waist.

A memory ripped through him—

His arm around Emily's waist in the same way, when she was learning to walk again. In a flash, he saw her face, heard her voice.

But it was Leah's head on his shoulder, her body liquid and nearly weightless in his arms. Her eyes were closed, and beads of perspiration stood out on her pale forehead. Her skin, when his hand brushed it, was icy cold.

Fear stabbed him. Was she... still breathing? "*Leah?*"

Time slowed, each second stretching into terrifying uncertainty.

Ana was already next to him, reaching for Leah. "*Careful!* Don't let her fall."

Kai held Leah tightly to him. Her head still rested on his shoulder, her mouth inches from his neck. But no air brushed his skin. "She's not—she's not..." He couldn't bring himself to say it.

Others drew near, anxious expressions on their faces. Riko, Zip, Hans, Ivy, Axer, Brie.

Ana pressed her hand over Leah's lips, and a sob shook her. "*Quick.* Lay her down." She helped him lower Leah to the floor.

"What's happening?" Kai asked.

"Hold her head," Ana directed, reaching inside a long pocket on the side of her pant leg.

Val burst in the door. "*Leah!*" Anguish rang in his voice. He rushed toward them, dragging his bad leg.

"I've got it, Val!" Ana called to him.

A small metal box flashed in her hands. She cracked it open, pulled out a syringe already loaded with a drug, and snapped off the safety.

"Then do it! Do it!" Val urged. "What are you waiting for?"

Ana looked at him. "It's the last one."

Val shuddered. "What? It can't be. Oh God." He closed his eyes. "Do it. We have no choice. Save her."

Ana slipped the needle into Leah's limp arm and injected the drug.

A spasm went through Leah's body, and her eyes popped open. She gasped for air, her chest rising and falling rapidly, before it slowed to a normal speed. She closed her eyes again, but she was breathing. Resting.

"Let me..." Val dropped to his knees next to Kai and gathered Leah into his own arms. Tears rolled down the fierce man's face and into his sister's hair.

Ana took Leah's hand in hers. But she didn't cry. She sat still like a statue, staring into space.

Kai got up and moved a few feet away, taking in the

scene. It didn't seem real. It couldn't be.

Leah's heart had stopped.

He didn't need medical training to get that.

The empty syringe lay on the floor. The *last* one. Not a drop left of the drug that brought her back to life.

What if she needed it again?

She would die.

No.

He almost said it out loud. The thought sounded like an explosion in his head.

Another thought followed. *The drug.*

They needed to get more of it for Leah.

And fast.

19
KAI

KAI WAITED OUTSIDE Leah's room for hours, hoping to talk to Val. Leah was in bed, conscious but very weak, and Val and Ana didn't leave her side. No one else was allowed in.

An aura of gratitude mixed with apprehension hung over the house. A horrible disaster had been narrowly avoided. People talked in hushed voices and took care not to stomp, as if afraid that any noise, any disturbance, could shatter the safety and bring the horror back.

When the door to Leah's room finally opened, it was Ana, and not Val, who emerged.

She threw Kai a cold glance and headed down the hallway.

Kai followed her without hesitation. "How is she?"

"Alive." Ana walked fast, looking straight ahead.

Desperation strangled Kai, and he grabbed her arm. "Wait. That drug saved her life. If it was the last dose, we need to get more!"

Ana spun toward him. "You think I don't know that?" She shook off his hand. "What do you care, anyway?"

Kai was taken aback. "You all voted for me to stay. Which means I'm part of the group. And I want to help."

"Do you really?" Ana's eyes bore into his. "You're sure you're not just going to take off? It's like you're only half present, anyway."

Kai frowned. "What are you talking about? I'm not

going anywhere."

"No? So who's *Emily?*"

Kai stared at her, stunned. "What? How do you know about her?" He'd never mentioned Emily to anyone in the group.

"You say her name in your sleep," Ana hissed the words at him.

"Emily is... She's... She *was*..." He couldn't talk about Emily. Not to Ana. It was none of her business. "What does it matter? This isn't about *me*. It's about *Leah*."

"Right." Ana scowled at him. "You know what your problem is? You need to figure out what you want. Until you do, stay away from Leah. Because if you hurt her, I swear..." And with that, she turned and stormed away without waiting for him to respond.

It was like a punch to the gut. Hurt Leah? What was that crazy woman talking about? He would never hurt Leah. He wanted her to get better. And he was going to prove it.

Kai found Green asleep at his computer. Green's cheek rested on his forearm, and his thick glasses had slid all the way down his nose. One hand was still on the keyboard, as if he'd crashed in the middle of typing.

Kai touched the mouse, and the screen came to life. A browser window appeared. But it wasn't the Boards, with their inverted colors. It was a regular website. A flashy product description of some sort.

Kai scrolled up—and froze.

The product was... an artificial heart.

And not just any heart. The sleek, new model they'd seen in the creepy advertisement on TV.

The Titan SI 200, manufactured and sold by his former Sponsor, 3D Electronics.

Kai's thoughts raced to Leah, and fear surged through him again.

"Green." Kai shook the boy's arm. "Green, wake up!"

"What?" Green lifted his head and fumbled with his glasses, blinking. "Kai? What's happening?"

"Talk to me," Kai demanded. "I want to know how we're going to help Leah. How we're going to save her!"

Green's eyes widened. "Val told you?"

"No. Nobody told me anything. That's the problem." Kai couldn't keep the accusation out of his voice. "I had to watch her nearly die today to figure it out."

"I heard." Green shuddered, then looked at the screen.

Kai followed his gaze. "Is that the plan? To get Leah an artificial heart? What about the drug? Isn't that easier?"

Green bit his lip, deciding. "Okay. I'll tell you what I know. But you can't repeat it to anyone."

"I swear. Now, what is it?"

Green swallowed hard. "The drug... is no good. I overheard Ana and Val talking about it. I mean, it helps for a while. But they've already used it several times, and it may not work the next time. They just don't know."

"*What?*" The room spun around Kai. "Leah's heart has stopped *several times?*"

Green nodded, a pained expression on his face. "Yeah. Once we almost lost her. Ana was out, and Val had to give her the injection himself, and the needle broke." He let out a shaky breath, remembering. "That's why Ana sticks to Leah. She always carries the drug on her. Well, I guess not anymore," he corrected himself. "Because we're out."

"Red sands," Kai said.

Leah needed a new heart—or she was going to die.

Kai turned his attention to the screen. Back to the sleek Titan SI 200. "So how much does one of those cost?"

Green reached for the mouse. "A lot? Nobody knows. You're supposed to consult with your doctor, if you have one. They don't list the price anywhere. See?" He scrolled through the page to demonstrate. "But I've heard rumors..." He broke off and chewed on his lip.

"What rumors?"

Green's shoulders stooped. "That the price is so high no one can afford it."

Kai frowned. "That doesn't make sense. If no one can afford it, then how would they make money?"

Green looked grim. "I mean, no one can afford to *buy* it. To pay the whole price all at once. But they can pay... per month."

Kai's stomach clenched. "You mean, like a *lease?* Like on a couch or a TV?" He thought of all the 3D printed furniture and appliances that got carted off from his house after his parents died and he could no longer make the payments. He was pissed, but he learned to do without them. But a heart... He shook his head. "No way. That can't be right."

Green dropped his gaze. "Maybe not. I don't know. It's just a rumor. Best not to repeat it to the others." Then he quickly added, "Anyway, Val will figure something out. We've been saving all the Collector money."

The Collector money!

Kai jumped from his chair.

That was it! He was going to save Leah.

He knew a Collector, a wealthy and powerful one. If she could afford the item he and Val delivered the other day, this would be nothing for her.

"Kai, where are you going?" Green called in a low voice, not to wake up the others. "We have a curfew now, remember? Nobody goes out after dark."

But Kai was already halfway down the stairs.

Outside, he ran for two hours without stopping, his prosthetic feet carrying him almost on their own.

Until he stood at the foot of the luxury building, looking up at the drifting smog that concealed the top twenty floors, the roof, and the airborne residence of the Collector above it.

The problem was how to get up there. He had neither a hovercraft nor an invitation, and it was the middle of the night.

But Kai was desperate. "Dr. Livingstone!" he yelled into the air. "Dr. Livingstone, I need to talk to you!" He craned his neck to look up.

He didn't have to wait long. A hovercraft dropped from the night sky and sped down along the wall of the building, straight toward him. For a moment, he thought it would flatten him into the pavement. But he planted his prosthetic feet firmly on the ground and didn't budge.

The hovercraft stopped barely an arm's length away from him. The hot air hit his face like a fist, and he coughed, blinking.

The door slid open, and the familiar security guard stepped outside. "What the hell do you think you're doing?" His hand was on the stun gun strapped to his thigh. "Do you have a death wish?"

A dozen insolent comebacks itched on Kai's tongue, but he swallowed them all down. It wouldn't do to provoke this man right now. It wouldn't help Leah. "I need to talk to your boss. It's important."

The security guard scowled. "You really are out of your mind."

"I have a business proposition for her." Kai spoke loudly, his eyes on the com link in the man's ear. "Trust me. She'll want to hear it."

The guard grabbed his gun and pointed it at Kai. "Okay. That's it—"

Every muscle in Kai's body screamed for him to run, to escape the pain that was coming, but he forced himself to stay put. "A Collector's item! One of a kind!" he yelled out.

Abruptly, the guard straightened. "Yes, madam. Right away." He gave Kai a murderous look and pointed with his gun toward the hovercraft. "Get in."

The ride was even shorter than last time, the hovercraft rushing upward with a speed that felt like a rock slamming into him, threatening to split his skull and crush his lungs.

Dr. Livingstone looked perfectly polished and unfazed when the guard ushered Kai into her office. She sat behind her desk, working on a pile of papers. Her cane stood next to her.

She finished reading a document and added her signature to the bottom before looking up. "Mr. Reed. I must say your visit is rather unexpected."

"I'm sorry to..." He was going to say, *wake you*, but the old lady gave no impression of having slept. Did she sleep at all? "I'm sorry to bother you. But I have an urgent... *business* to discuss with you." The word stuck in his throat.

The old woman put down the pen and regarded him. "Something about a Collector's item? Did I hear that correctly?"

Kai swallowed. "That's right."

"Go on. I'm listening."

Kai's muscles tensed almost to breaking, his whole body again screaming at him to turn and run, to forget what he was about to do and get away.

But he couldn't. Leah needed his help.

"A friend of mine is very sick." He could barely recognize his voice. "Her heart... is failing."

"I am very sorry to hear that." The Collector studied him with cool detachment, and for a moment a wild suspicion passed through Kai's head. She already knew why he was here. She already knew what he was going to ask. But she wanted to hear him say it anyway. Like a test of some sort.

"She needs a new heart." Cold sweat slicked his skin and his pulse drummed in his ears as if he'd been running. "Without a new heart, she'll die."

"I see." He had hoped for sympathy, but Olympia Livingstone was unmoved, and now there was a note of displeasure in her voice, as if he had let her down somehow. "And what is it that you think I can do for you, Mr. Reed?"

A footstep sounded in the hallway, and Kai shuddered. He had to get to the point, or he would run out of time. This was his only chance.

"There's an artificial heart that could save her life." He spoke hurriedly. "But it's expensive, and we can't afford it. So I'm here to offer you a deal." A wave of sickness crawled up his throat, but he fought it down. He took a deep breath and extended his left arm. "My arm... for your collection."

Slowly, the old woman rose from her desk. She was much smaller than him, her frame fragile, her bones as brittle as glass. But somehow, even leaning on her cane, she towered over Kai, proud and untouchable. "That's a very generous offer. But I'm afraid I must turn it down."

Despair and relief waged a battle in Kai's chest. "Why?"

"Oh, I don't object to your price. Frankly, money is not a concern." Her tone was matter-of-fact. "And the item would add immeasurable value to my collection. No doubt about that." She took a step toward him and pushed his extended arm down with her cane, refusing the offering. "*But* I cannot permit you to use the money as you intend."

Kai stared at her in confusion. "I don't... follow."

"I know this isn't easy. These things never are." The old woman lifted her chin. "But I cannot help you. It goes against everything I believe. It's a matter of principle."

"What principle is that?" Kai choked out, taking a step forward. "She's going to die!"

The guard was next to him a flash. But the old woman waved him away.

"As I told you before." The old woman regarded Kai sternly. "I am a biologist, and I believe in the wisdom of Nature. Nature may be cruel, but it is still wise. Not like a person is wise, but in a way that was shaped by endless trial and error, until it arrived at a solution that works best." She continued in a chilly tone, her gaze piercing through Kai with stern disapproval. "It is the highest measure of human arrogance to think, even for a moment, that we can improve on Nature."

She glanced at a wedding photograph of a young, happy couple on the wall. "Oh, it may seem like we know better, like we can outsmart Nature for a while, like we can bend the rules and escape our own limitations. But trust me when I tell you, it's an illusion. We're fooling ourselves. All we do is interfere and cause even greater damage, even greater suffering, later on."

Kai's mind reeled. This rich woman was sending him out the door empty-handed because of some abstract idea. "So you're saying she should die? And I should just... accept it?"

"Yes."

"No!" Kai shook his head. "What if it was *you?* What if your heart was failing right now?"

The Collector narrowed her eyes. "When my time comes, I will accept death without protest."

Kai watched her in bitter defeat. It was over.

"You say you care about what makes us *human.* But you don't." The words burned on his lips. "All you care about is *body parts.* And we're more than that. I'm more than my legs, or my arms, or the rest of my body. You're missing what really matters." He shook his head. "You don't see human beings. You see machines."

The Collector's face changed, her mouth gasping for air and her eyes momentarily wide with shock. But she collected herself quickly. "I believe our conversation is over." She turned away, dismissing him. "Goodbye, Mr. Reed. I do not expect we will speak again."

Kai had to will his legs to move, his heart heavy like a stone.

20
KAI

"DON'T COME BACK," the guard warned Kai when the hovercraft dropped down to the street level.

Kai climbed out and stalked away without a word. He had caught a glimpse of pity in the man's eyes. It was worse than if he had threatened him.

Leah isn't going to die! Kai wanted to scream in the guard's face. *I won't let that happen!* But what would be the point? And how exactly was he going to save her?

He started walking. At night, the streets of the business district were even more lifeless than in daylight, and he was grateful for that. He was disgusted with the entire human race right now. A helpless fury ripped through him each time the Collector's words echoed in his mind.

Money is not a concern.

Money is not a concern.

Then why not save Leah's life? The frustration tore at him.

As if to mock him, a drone flying along the opposite side of the street paused and rotated in the air. The camera aimed straight at Kai. Someone was watching him. Maybe laughing at him.

Kai glared at the drone, his good hand itching for a rock to throw. But that would be stupid. He wasn't even wearing a mask. So he forced himself to look down and keep moving.

He kept on walking, automatically retracing his steps back to the house, while angry, desperate thoughts swarmed in his mind like crazed insects.

What was wrong with this world? The medical technology could end almost any illness and fix any injury to the human body. But the prices were so steep that only the rich benefited. The poor were left to die.

The Collector wanted to convince him that it was the right order of things because Nature was wise. But Kai didn't buy it. It wasn't Nature that decided who lived or died anymore. It was money. The Collector had to be a hundred years old, and apart from her walking cane, she looked to be in good health. Why? Because she was rich. Protected. Eating good food, breathing good air.

When Leah wasn't even twenty and her weak heart could kill her at any moment.

The memory of his friend's pale face sent another wave of helpless anger through Kai. But this time, he was angry at himself. He was a Runner. He got to the final day of the Race. Where was his reward? Where was his money? He should be rich!

But the anger dissipated quickly.

He *had* been rich at one point, and if he had held on to the money, it would have lasted him a long time. But he had chosen to share it with people he cared about, people who needed it more than he did, although they would never have asked him for it.

He thought of Ron, Sam, and Sara. When he went back to his hometown after the Race, he had seen the difference the money made. His friends' lives had transformed overnight. The Ghost Street brought back to life. Kai only wished he had more to give them.

And Emily...

How could he ever regret the money he gave her? Or not exactly gave her, since she would never have accepted the gift. A surgery that brought back her ability to walk. He had to be cunning and trick her into accepting it before she even knew it was from him.

The image of Emily learning to walk again, snapping at the nurse to let her do it on her own, brought a smile to Kai's face.

No, he could never regret how he spent the money from the Race. If he went back in time, he would make the same choices all over again. He just wished Runners earned more for racing...

An idea went off in his head. It wasn't new, and it brought memories of agonizing pain. But he clutched at it with desperate eagerness.

Runners *could* earn more! They could race in *cage races!*

Kai had no idea what time it was, but if he hurried, maybe he could get into one tonight.

He broke into a run.

When he reached his destination, the abandoned factory building looked as desolate as ever, with its cracked walls and boarded up windows. But the street was far from empty despite the late hour. People hurried toward the building from all directions, some in groups, some alone. A faint echo of shouting voices and stomping feet came from inside the walls.

A race was about to start.

Kai halted and watched from across the street, his feet frozen in place. The memories were so vivid, he could feel the pain in his legs—his nerves ripped and muscles crushed, while his prostheses became a twisted, burning pile of electronic junk.

But he had no choice. He needed the money. Leah had saved his life. He had to repay her.

So he shook himself, crossed the street, and followed a stream of people to the back entrance.

A roar of voices hit him when he entered.

The observation deck that stretched along the walls was already packed with fans, and they were impatient for the show to begin. A new, stronger wire cage enclosed the robotic assembly line converted into an obstacle track. The other viewing spaces around the cage were quickly filling up. The air in the massive factory hall was thick with the odors of sweat and machine oil.

Kai peered over the line of people that had formed in front of him.

Up ahead, Ronny wove his way through the crowd, chatting up the regulars and collecting bets. He spotted Kai and came over, a wary look on his face. "What do *you* want?"

"I want to race."

"You want to race, huh? You think it's that easy?" Ronny scowled at him. "You cost me a lot of money in repairs last time. Remember that? And did you offer to help cover any of it? No, you didn't! And now you come crawling back, asking me to let you race again. And let me guess, you hope to win and take off with all the cash? Is that your plan?"

Normally, Kai wouldn't give anything that came out of Ronny's mouth a second thought. But today his mockery almost pushed him over the edge. "Yes, you *weasel!* That's exactly my plan! Now are you going to let me race, or not?"

Ronny's eyes narrowed at the insult. "What did you just call me?" He pointed to the exit. "Get out of here, or I'll throw you out!"

Kai started to turn. "Forget it. I'll find another race."

But a heavy hand dropped on Ronny's shoulder, nearly knocking him to his knees.

"Let him race," Death Wish said, his half-mangled face twisting in a menacing grin. His good eye stayed on Kai. "Hell, make him a special attraction. Didn't you say he's a Runner? Folks will eat it up."

"But—"

"Don't worry. I can handle him." Death Wish slammed the manager on the back. "Call it a rematch. Winner takes all. You can keep my share."

A shrewd and calculating look lit up Ronny's face. "Fine. You're in," he told Kai. "But you heard the new rules?"

Kai wasn't thrilled with Ronny announcing he was a Runner. But he couldn't back out now. "I heard them." He looked Death Wish in the eye. " *'Winner takes all'* suits me fine. And I'll be keeping my share."

Kai and Death Wish followed Ronny inside the cage, where three other runners already waited. They all nodded to Death Wish and glared at Kai. He didn't recognize any of them.

With big profits on the horizon, Ronny threw himself into action. "Ladies and Gentlemen!" he yelled into his microphone. "Or should I say—Fellow Citizen of the Alliance!"

A hush fell over the massive hall, people turning to one another in surprise at the familiar address. Everybody knew and watched the Race. Everybody felt the same shiver of excitement.

Pleased with the reaction, Ronny proceeded with his announcement. "Tonight's cage race will be the most spectacular you've ever seen. Why? Because tonight one of the runners is raising the stakes for all the others. He brings training and experience from the most extreme Race on the planet."

Wild screams of excitement shook the hall, and Ronny beamed at the audience.

"That's right! This Runner competed in a Global No Limits Race! And in a moment, you will see him compete in a winner-takes-all showdown against our own, fierce and unbeatable, *Death Wish!"*

A cross of shifting laser beams appeared, and Death Wish stepped into it, pumping his arms in victory.

"Death Wish! Death Wish!" The whole building shook with the crowd's chanting and stomping boots, and the new wire cage rattled under their pounding fists.

Ronny's enthusiasm momentarily faltered as he saw his new cage so abused, but he put on a bright smile and continued. "And now, for the main attraction of tonight's race, I give you the world-famous, technologically-enhanced Runner from last year's No Limits Race—*Sand Runner!"*

The laser lights hit Kai from above just as he spun to Ronny, blinking in shock.

What?

He wasn't supposed to give Kai's name away—only that he had been a Runner in the Race.

Ronny caught his eye and scowled, as if to say, *Don't like it? Too bad.*

Meanwhile, the audience was divided, half of them cheering, the other half booing.

Ronny frowned. He needed the crowd to warm up to his main attraction if he was to make his desired profits. "Sand Runner!" he yelled. "Come on! Show them what you've got!" He gestured at a nearby stamping press, a massive structure nearly two stories high that had once pressed sheets of steel into car frames.

Kai assessed the obstacle. Then he squared his shoulders, leaned forward, and set off.

He ran three steps—and leapt at the machine, landing halfway up. Two more running steps, and he was on top. Another leap—and his prosthetic feet hit the ground a good ten yards behind the press.

There was a collective gasp—and then the crowd exploded into applause.

"Sand Runner, everyone! His robotic legs give him

superhuman speed!" Ronny yelled. "Place your bets! Place your bets!"

People rushed down from the observation deck and crowded around. Ronny stepped back outside the cage to collect the bets. He could barely keep up with the money that was pushed at him.

One man, in an expensive, fashionable suit with an insect print, nearly stomped over other people in his rush to place the bet. "Sand Runner!" he told Ronny, pressing a whole wad of cash into his hand. "All of it on Sand Runner! He *has* to win!"

Ronny grinned at the man, pocketing the cash and giving out a stub for the bet.

But Kai watched with unease.

There was something odd about the man in the insect-print suit. He looked painfully out of place here. People threw him dark, envious looks as he passed them, sizing him up in ways that should make him nervous. But he seemed oblivious.

When the bets were placed, Ronny and Death Wish exchanged a look through the wire wall of the cage. Ronny hurried to a control panel on the wall and flipped a series of switches.

Bright lights flooded the obstacle track that looped around the factory floor. Except it wasn't a clear, wide path anymore. All along it, hissing and whirring machines jerked to life. Robotic arms reached and grabbed, nozzles ignited with sparks, conveyor belts sped forward, rams inside stamping presses slammed into their dies.

The runners lined up at the start line.

"You're dead, Sand Runner." Death Wish sneered.

Kai ignored him, scanning the track ahead. The machines moved at a frantic pace, some twice as fast as he remembered. Was Ronny trying to kill all the runners? No matter. Kai had speed to match. But he had to stay sharp, too. No distractions this time, no mistakes. He couldn't win if he was dead.

The start signal sounded—and time suddenly sped up.

Twenty seconds into the race, Kai was firmly in the lead. He sprinted faster and leapt further than he ever had while dodging the robots that threatened to cut, smash, or burn him.

Memories of other races pushed into his mind, but he shut them out. The audience screamed his name and rattled the cage around him, but he blocked the sounds.

There was only the next stretch of the track to run, the next machine to dodge or leap over. There was only this one race to win. Nothing else mattered.

He was ahead of Death Wish but always aware of him. The other three runners fell far behind.

Kai had just rounded a corner, risking a glance behind him, when an oversized gripper swung at him from the right.

He veered to the left, forced to slow down, just as a row of spraying nozzles dropped over his head. He raised his left arm for protection—and one nozzle dug into his hand.

The pain nailed him to the place, and he struggled to dislodge the nozzle, finally breaking it off. Blood poured from his hand where the sharp metal ripped his flesh, and he stared at it in horror.

By the time he heard footsteps behind him, it was too late.

Death Wish shoved him in the back, and Kai tripped and nearly fell, slamming his shoulder against the side of a stamping press. He dodged a gripper reaching inside the die, then raced around the press.

With nowhere to go and Death Wish right behind him, Kai gathered speed and leapt over a wide conveyor belt. His prosthetic heel touched the speeding metal, but he made it across.

He expected Death Wish to follow him. But he was nowhere in sight.

Then Kai saw him. Trapped and dragged along the conveyor belt toward the same scrap metal disposal that nearly ripped Kai in half last time.

Panic showed in the one-eyed man's face as he frantically tried to free himself.

Kai had about a second to decide.

Finish the race and win the money? Or save this man from certain death?

It was no decision at all. He was already racing along the conveyor belt. A gripper reached for him, and he grabbed it and tore it from the base. The motor sat near the end of the conveyor. Kai slid to the floor and kicked at it until the lid flew off. Then he jammed the gripper into the motor.

The motor emitted a shrill grinding noise—and the conveyor belt stopped.

"Ladies and Gentlemen!" Ronny's voice boomed from the speakers, "And here is the first runner to cross the finish line. We have a winner! I repeat, we have a winner! And it's not Sand Runner *or* Death Wish! Wow! Just—*wow!* Nobody could have predicted that! What a spectacular conclusion to a spectacular race!"

Disappointment slammed into Kai.

Death Wish slid off the conveyor belt and got to his feet. He was limping, his right arm and leg bloodied, his clothes torn. He looked at Kai and opened his mouth. Then closed it.

Kai turned and walked out of the cage. Out of the building. He looked at no one, although he felt their eyes on him.

On the street, the man in the insect-print suit grabbed his arm. He had run after him. His eyes were wild. "You've killed me!" He dug his nails into Kai's flesh, his face twisted and spit flying from his mouth. "I'm dead! Do you hear me? I'm a dead man!"

"You're crazy! I didn't do anything to you!" Kai yanked his arm free. "Leave me alone!" He had saved a life, not taken one.

But he watched the man until he disappeared down the street, and guilt ate at him.

What would happen to Leah now?

21
EMILY

EMILY WAS ASLEEP on the sofa when Xander's voice woke her. "Em! Come take a look at this!"

She rubbed her eyes and glanced around. Outside the windows, gray dawn broke over the city, the rays of the rising sun trapped in the smog.

"Why did you let me fall asleep?" She scowled at him as she walked over.

But Xander only grinned and pointed at the hologram in front of him. "Look!"

Emily squinted at the 3D image, and her eyes lit up. "The database! It's not shifting!"

"Nope. Not by itself. Now we can control it." Xander slipped his hands into the hologram and brought them closer together, zooming out until the entire structure was visible, as if from a distance. He started slowly rotating the structure left to right. "So what do you want to search for? Any specific type of file?"

Emily took a deep breath. Her heart was pounding, hope battling with fear of what she would find. "Patient files. Medical histories. Treatment schedules."

"Treatment schedules?" Xander sounded surprised. But his fingers were already signing instructions into the projected screen.

Emily watched, transfixed, as one section of the database moved to the foreground, filling the screen, then kept growing larger until they were inside it. Files flew from the virtual shelves and merged into one document, which split open, text and numbers scrolling on the screen with dizzying speed.

Xander frowned. "The omnibus file is huge. Can you narrow down the search?"

She hesitated. He already knew too much. What if he put it all together?

Xander studied her. "You came to me for help, but you still don't trust me."

"It's not about trust. It's about the risk."

"I can handle the risk," he said.

Emily turned to the hologram. The information was still scrolling across the screen. Xander was right. The file *was* huge.

For a moment, panic gripped her. Why was the file so big? It shouldn't be. The device was still new. How many patients were there?

But it wasn't the number of patients. It was the sheer amount of data on each one, starting with their full genome.

"Fine," she told Xander. "Then search for payment schedules. Payments that are *late*."

Xander didn't move for a moment, as if waiting for an explanation. Then his hands moved.

Just as smaller files had flown together before, merging into an omnibus file, now the process was reversed, and the large document broke apart, information flying off into the background, until a much smaller file was left. Now only spreadsheets scrolled across the virtual screen.

"Can you arrange them by date?" Emily asked.

"What date is that?"

"Try... *termination* date." The word choked her. It meant murder. A cold, calculated, precisely timed murder.

Xander watched her, his strange, mismatched eyes full of concern. "I don't like this."

Emily held his gaze. "I don't like it either," she said. "It's wrong, and it has to stop. That's the whole point."

Xander had put it together. The artificial heart, the payment schedules, the termination dates. She could see it in his eyes.

"I meant, I don't like that *you* are mixed up in it," came the correction. It was the new Xander talking.

"I know what you meant. But it's not your decision. It's mine."

"Okay." His fingers resumed signing into the hologram. A moment later, a spreadsheet filled the screen. A patient file. "Here's the nearest date."

Emily moved closer. "When?"

Xander zoomed in. He swallowed. "It's... today."

"What? *No!"* Emily gripped Xander's arm, digging her nails in. But she quickly let go, collecting herself. She scanned the information.

At least the file listed both the name and the address.

Victor Harding, age 42, lived in a luxury condo on the edge of the business district.

It wasn't far. She could still make it. If she could get him to Neen, maybe she would know what to do, and the man still had a chance...

Emily crossed the room and grabbed her coat and backpack from the sofa.

"Em! Where are you going? This is crazy!" Xander blocked her way. "You *can't* help him!"

But Emily pushed past him. "I have to try."

She ran down the stairs, shrugging on her coat, then her backpack.

Sylvia had died even though Emily had Kai's jacket with her, and the jacket blocked the wireless signal. So Titan SI 200 wasn't turned off remotely. But then, how was it turned off?

She still had no idea. But she trusted in Neen's ability to figure it out and fix it.

Downstairs, she put on her mask and lifted her hood, then pushed outside and broke into a run. She raced down the street, her eyes stinging as much from frustration as from the acrid air.

Titan SI 200 was flawless. It was meant to keep a person alive for two hundred years. Neen had said that herself. No matter how cunning the switch, there had to be a way to keep the heart beating despite it.

Soon, the skyscrapers of the business district towered over Emily, their top floors shrouded in smog. It was still early morning. In another hour, the air would be filled with hover cabs carrying executives from their high-rise condos to their high-rise offices only a few blocks away.

She reached Victor's apartment building and stood across the street, unsure of what to do next. She knew nothing about the man, but at the same time, knew altogether too much. What could she say to him? Would he even agree to see her, or would he simply send the building security to have her arrested?

She was looking up, trying to imagine which floor he lived on, when movement caught her eye.

A man stepped out of the entrance and headed down the street. He looked disheveled despite his expensive-looking insect-print suit, as if he hadn't showered or changed his clothes for days.

It was him! Victor Harding.

"Mr. Harding!" she called out, crossing the street toward him.

The man froze, staring at her. Then he spun around and dashed into the alley that flanked the building.

"No—*wait!*" Emily ran after him.

The man ran awkwardly, obviously unused to it. Then he halted. A shudder went through his body, and he leaned against the wall, clutching his left side.

Emily froze. *Not again.* First Sylvia, and now this man.

The man turned his head and watched her in horror.

She pulled off her mask so he could see her face. "It's okay," she said, drawing closer. "I'm a friend. I'm not here to hurt you."

But the man shook his head. "No, no, no. I'll get the money. I swear it. I just need more time. My next commission will be big. Enough for six months!" He shuddered again, folding into himself. "*Please.*"

Emily stepped closer. "I want to help you. Have the people who gave you the heart mentioned a switch? Try to remember—"

"You can't take it away!" The man suddenly lunged forward and punched her clumsily in the mouth.

Emily staggered backward, tasting blood. The man's fist had split her lip.

A security drone appeared in the mouth of the alley. It patrolled the main street.

Emily lowered her head, letting the hood hide her face, as she waited for it to pass.

When she looked up again, Victor was gone.

"No." She hurried down the alley after him.

Another alley crossed it up ahead, and Emily quickly scanned it, turning to her right. But it looked empty, no sign of movement anywhere.

Then she heard a gasp.

It came from the alley on the left, and Emily ran in that direction.

Victor lay on the ground, his eyes open and staring, arms spread to the sides, and one knee bent at an unnatural angle, as if his legs had buckled under him.

He was dead.

Emily sunk to her knees next to him.

Victor's shirt was torn open at the throat. A metal ID

showed under his left collar bone, just like the one Sylvia had. The numbers were brightly lit when her heart was beating, then turned dark after it stopped.

Now Victor's ID was dark as well.

You can't take it away!

He had yelled the words at her in desperation, as if she was going to rip the heart out of his chest and carry it away.

But now a terrible thought struck her.

That was exactly what she should do. What she had to do. The design diagrams would never tell her everything.

Emily lifted her hands to the man's chest—and quickly withdrew them.

Nausea churned in the pit of her stomach. She couldn't do it. It was too horrific. She'd have to be... a monster.

But time was running out. Kai's jacket in her backpack masked the dead man's location. But a team was already on the way to retrieve the body and the data. It wouldn't take them long to find an alley next to his apartment building.

Emily bit her lip, tasting blood again. Her mind screamed for her to get up, to move, to get out of there.

But she couldn't walk away. This could be her only chance to learn how the switch worked and how to disable it. She thought of the long list of people who were late on their payments. She had no choice. What she was about to do was monstrous, but it was the only way.

"Forgive me," she whispered, and she pulled the man's shirt open.

With the pocket knife from her backpack, she made a cut down his chest. The flesh around the surgery scar gave way more easily than she had expected, and a moment later, she reached in and pulled out the artificial heart. Tubes came trailing behind it, and she snapped them off, her hands shaking now.

Blood poured from the dead man's chest like a river. Emily quickly wrapped the heart in Kai's jacket and stuffed it into her backpack.

She got to her feet, now shaking all over, and backed away from the body, to where the alleys crossed. She heard a noise behind her and spun around, half expecting the team with the stretcher to be running toward her from the main street. But the alley was still empty.

On unsteady legs, she ran down the alley, away from the main street, away from what she had done.

I'm a monster. I'm a monster. I'm a monster.

The thought echoed in her head all the way to Neen's door.

This time Neen herself let her in. Her gaze slipped down Emily's arms. "You have blood on your hands."

Emily felt lightheaded. Yes, she had blood on her hands. Neen had no idea.

"It's not mine." She slipped off her backpack. It was stained with blood as well. "I have something to show you. But I need a table."

Neen was never bothered by the sight of blood. She led her into a work room. "Here."

Emily pulled out Kai's jacket. There was blood on it too, but only on the surface. The fabric didn't absorb it. "The jacket blocks the tracking device. We should keep it close."

Neen waved her hand. "No need. The walls already block all wireless signals." She was clearly impatient to see what was inside.

Emily unfolded the jacket and produced the artificial heart.

Neen's eyes lit up, and she came closer. "The new Titan." She grabbed a towel and started to wipe the blood off the device. She must have known that the heart came out of a person, and quite recently, but she asked no questions. Her attention was on the device itself.

"Remember the diagrams I brought you? I don't think they showed everything. I know the heart has a switch—"

Neen turned to her. "What switch? I already told you. The Titan has no switch."

"But it must have one." Emily's hands shook at the memories. Maybe *a switch* wasn't the right word? "Whatever you want to call it. I've seen what it does!"

Neen shook her head. "You're mistaken. Titan SI 200 comes powered for two hundred years. Plus, all systems are capable of robust self-monitoring and self-adjustment. Once the device is charged and activated, there is no way to turn it off... except to rip it out of someone's chest."

Blood drained from Emily's face. "He was already dead. I swear it. I would never—"

"I believe you," Neen said simply. "Now I want to examine the heart. I'll let you know if I discover anything unusual."

Emily sighed in frustration. This was her cue to leave. Part of her wanted to shake Neen and scream at her to hurry up. This was urgent, people were going to die! But that wouldn't work. Neen couldn't be rushed. Besides, Emily had no other ideas.

She glanced at her blood-stained clothes and backpack. "Do you mind if I use your bathroom to clean up?" Her stuff could go in the laundry while she scrubbed the blood off herself in the shower.

"Sure. Over there." Neen waved her hand toward the hallway without looking up.

22
EMILY

XANDER WAS WAITING for her when she got back. He frowned when he saw her face and took a step toward her. "Are you okay? What happened?"

Emily's hand automatically went to her swollen lip. She had forgotten all about it. "Nothing." She slipped past him into the apartment. "I'm fine."

Her clothes and backpack were clean, all the blood stains removed. Inside the backpack, securely wrapped in Kai's jacket, was the artificial heart. She hadn't planned to bring the device near Xander, but here it was.

Neen had taken the heart apart for study and then put it back together. As she had been saying all along, Titan SI 200 had no switch of any kind. Although Neen puzzled over the battery, which was unfamiliar to her and gave strange readings when tested with her equipment.

It was Andy who had pressed the device back into Emily's hands when the Print Maker had stepped out of the room and told her in no gentle terms to take it and get out, or they would all end up in jail. Emily didn't argue. Andy was protective of Neen, but he had also worked for Falcon. Who knew where his loyalty really lay? Andy was a difficult man to read.

Xander peered into her face. "Do you want to tell me—?"

"There's nothing to tell," she said angrily, walking

away from him. "He's dead. I couldn't do anything to help him. You were right." She just wanted to get to the bedroom and close the door.

"There *is* something you can do," said Xander.

She stopped and turned toward him. "Oh yeah? What's that?"

"The Boards."

She was speechless for a moment. "I thought you didn't believe in them." She couldn't keep bitterness out of her voice.

Xander didn't blink. "But *you* do."

"And what would I post, exactly? An obituary?"

But Xander responded in earnest. "I thought you wanted to warn people. So that's what you could post—a *warning*."

That touched a nerve in her. "You think it's that easy? Do you know how many times I've tried? You have no idea!" The old frustration surged through her. She had tried posting again and again, until she had to give up or go crazy. "I can't post anything on the Boards! All right? There's something wrong with my account!"

Xander turned thoughtful. "You mean, you can read other people's messages, but your own messages disappear right after you post them?"

"That's right. As soon as I post anything—it's gone!" She had tried and tried to figure out the problem, until she'd given up.

"But they're all *text* messages, right?" Xander pressed. "And maybe *photos?*"

"No photos. Just—words." Emily was getting irritated. All her messages were text. How else could she communicate her meaning? "Why?"

"I have an idea that might work," Xander said cautiously. "But... you're not going to like it."

She just looked at him and waited.

"You could try posting a video."

A suspicion chilled her. *"What video?"*

"I saw what happened to Victor."

Emily shuddered and took a step back, her hands gripping the straps of her backpack. "You... *saw?"*

"Through a drone. But you wouldn't have seen it. I kept it out of view."

It was like the air was suddenly sucked out of the room. She couldn't catch her breath.

Xander had spied on her. Again. He had seen what she'd done to Victor. And he also... recorded it?

"Nobody will recognize you," Xander assured her. "Your hood covers your face, and there's no audio. I would never suggest it if it wasn't safe. Besides, you would only post a short clip. Not... the whole thing." He watched her. "But it's totally up to you. We can destroy it if you want."

"No!" Emily found her voice again. "Don't destroy it. I want to see it."

Xander hesitated, then loaded his tablet into the docking station. "You ready?" he asked gently.

"Play it."

Emily braced herself for the worst, but the video in the hologram was nothing like what she remembered of the event.

For one, the angle was strange, with the camera in the air and pointing straight down. Victor was easier to recognize, with his bare head and distinctive suit. But in her dark, long coat, and with the hood covering her face, Emily could be anyone, man or woman.

The lack of audio further drained any emotion from the scene. Emily watched with detachment as Victor threw a silent punch at her own hooded figure.

To her surprise, the camera followed Victor, zooming in on him as he dashed into the alley on the left.

He didn't make it far before one knee buckled under

him, and he collapsed, falling flat on his back. He shuddered, his eyes bulging, hands clawing at his shirt. The camera zoomed even more, until Victor's thrashing body filled the frame. A metal ID blinked on Victor's chest. Then his arms splayed to the sides, and he went still. The metal ID turned dark.

Emily startled when a hooded figure entered the frame a moment later.

The figure sat motionless for what seemed like a long time. Then she reached out and touched the man's chest, a timid gesture of respect and grief. A strap of a backpack briefly came into view. Then the hands withdrew, and the hooded figure was gone.

Xander tapped the hologram, freezing the video. "That's it. We wouldn't show the rest. People may misunderstand."

Emily nodded, relived. "Okay."

"Just Victor's death and your... goodbye to him." Xander pulled up a video editor and was already selecting the frames of the clip. "It has to be short."

Emily watched numbly as he worked. But she roused herself when he opened a browser, and she was suddenly looking at the Boards, with its background dark and the messages light.

"Wait!" She moved closer. "We need words. An explanation."

Xander's hands hovered motionlessly while he thought. Then they sprang into action again. He opened another program and loaded the clip. Split it into several bands of data.

He turned to Emily. "Okay. What do you want to say? I'll embed the text right into the video."

Emily dug her nails into her palms. "I don't know... Hold on... Let me think..."

"It needs to hit them hard. Make them angry."

"How about this?" She cleared her throat. "*Listen to me. I am here to warn you. You have been lied to—*"

But Xander cut her off, "Stronger and more direct. Come on! *You* are angry too, remember?"

Emily glared at him. She *was* angry. So angry she could scream. "Fine! Write this then: *3D Electronics is lying to you! Titan SI 200 kills people! Spread the word and fight back!*"

Xander smiled. "That's better. Give me a second."

She watched transfixed as her words became a hologram inside the hologram, a somber, shifting graffiti passing through the scene.

An unfamiliar voice poured from the speakers. "3D Electronics is lying to you!" The voice changed from male to female. "Titan SI 200 *kills* people!" It changed again. "Spread the word and fight back!"

Emily glanced at Xander, her heartbeat quickening with the familiar admiration. It was almost like the old Xander was back.

And what would she do if he was?

"How's that?" he asked.

Emily dropped her gaze, her cheeks suddenly warm. "It's fine. Go ahead and post it."

"Me? Oh no. It's your message."

"But it won't work," Emily protested. "My posts are blocked. I told you."

Xander pulled up a code editor and made a quick change. "Try it."

Emily stepped closer. She started a new post and loaded the file. Her message appeared in the stream, the video set to autoplay.

She held her breath, waiting for it to vanish, as all her posts in the last year had done. But it didn't. And now a counter showed 1, then 3, then 8 views.

Her message was on the Boards, and people were seeing it!

A sense of power warmed her. She wasn't helpless after all. She could speak to people. She could share information. She could break the silence.

But instantly, doubt cut through her confidence. It was... too easy.

She turned to Xander. "What did you change just now?" she asked. "I didn't know we could even access the code for the Boards."

The lightness was gone from his face. "We can't."

"Then *what* did you change, Xander?" Emily repeated.

He didn't answer right away, just looked at her, and she suddenly wished she could take back the question. *No, don't tell me. I don't want to know.*

But she couldn't take it back. She *had* to know.

"It's a crawler program," Xander finally said. "It crawls through the Boards and removes specific posts. It also blocks the people who posted them."

"What kind of posts?"

"Any negative mentions of the company that paid for it. Text or images." He paused. "But *not* videos. That's what I just changed."

In a heartbeat, all warmth seeped out of Emily's body. She wrapped her arms around herself. "You wrote the program." It wasn't a question.

"Yes. I was hired to write it."

"And who hired you?"

Xander looked at her with his strange, unmatching eyes. As if he was two different people. "Why do you ask if you already know?"

"Because I want to hear you say it," Emily hissed the words.

She was wrong. This wasn't the old Xander. She could never hate the old Xander—her Xander—and she was very close to hating the one in front of her.

"Alright. 3D Electronics hired me."

Emily wrapped her arms more tightly around herself. But it made no difference. Her whole body was ice, not a breath of warmth left. *"Why?"*

Xander looked surprised. "Why? Because they want to protect their corporate image—"

"No!" Emily cried. "I don't give a damn about them! I want to know why *you* did it!"

Xander shrugged. "They paid me a fortune."

Emily lunged at him. "You liar! You traitor!" She hit his chest and shoulder with her fists, not really aiming, not really seeing through the tears. "You sold us out! The Boards were the only place where people could still learn the truth, and you took that away from us!"

Xander didn't move, letting her hit him.

"What happened to you?" She kept hitting him, but there was no anger left, only loss and disbelief. *"Syber* would never betray his people like that!"

Xander's face darkened. He caught her wrists. "Stop."

She yanked her hands free and glared at him.

"You want to know what happened to Syber? I got sick of him! Of being him. Of always trying to do the right thing. And for what?" Xander shook his head. "You think Syber was some powerful, revered leader that everyone would follow? *Wrong*. He was nobody. He talked and talked, and nobody listened. Nobody did anything. Nothing Syber ever did made any difference."

"That's not true," Emily said.

But Xander ignored her. "So one day I thought to myself, why am I doing this? What's the point?" His lips curled. "I don't owe them anything. I can't save them. I can't solve all their problems for them. They have to do it themselves. They have to work for it. Fight for it! Not just bow their heads and try to survive another day."

"But that's exactly why they need you. Why they need Syber!" Emily protested. "Syber showed them how to stand up for themselves and fight back. And he would never sell them out!"

Xander looked at her, his gaze piercing. "Then I'm *not* Syber! Maybe I never was. Maybe the real Syber is out there. But it's not me. I just... don't care anymore."

Emily looked away. "The program you wrote. How many posts did it remove? How many people did it block?"

"Hundreds. I don't know exactly. I haven't checked."

"You have to turn it off," she told him.

Xander was silent for a moment. "Will you stay if I do?"

Emily shook her head. She was already standing near the door. "No. I can't."

23
KAI

WITH THE REST of the repairs on the house completed—except the smashed electric fan, which could be neither fixed nor replaced—Kai spent most of his time working in the greenhouse under Leah's direction.

On the morning after the cage race, he had stood outside the house for nearly an hour, ashamed and torn about what to do. Twice now, he had set out to get money and failed, and he hated coming back empty-handed. But leaving, walking away from the group, would be even worse. Unthinkable.

So he had knocked on the door, and Hans let him in. He also bandaged Kai's injured hand without asking a single question. A double relief.

Later that morning, Val had thrown Kai a dark look when passing him on the stairs. But that was all.

Kai had to remind himself that his failure was secret. None of the others even knew about his attempts. He couldn't decide if that made it easier or harder. He would have liked to talk it over with someone, to unburden himself and move on, instead of dwelling on the disappointment.

He climbed the stairs to Green's room. Green was working on his computer when Kai entered. He hurriedly shut it down, almost knocking the mouse off the table. Kai caught a glimpse of a browser window and the inversed colors of the Boards.

"How's it going?" he asked.

"It's nothing," Green said, distractedly. He was thinner now than when Kai had first met him, his bulky lenses too large for his face. It looked like he had troubles and disappointments of his own.

Kai felt a stab of sympathy for his friend. "Don't worry, Green," he said. "We'll get Leah that new heart. We'll find a way." He needed to tell himself that, as much as anyone else.

Green paled and looked away. "I know." Then he slid off his chair and turned to the door, still not looking at Kai. "I... forgot I'm helping Zip today. I've got to go."

"Sure." Kai stepped aside to let him pass.

Maybe it was better that way. Maybe nobody needed to know about the Collector or the cage race. He would wait until he had good news to share. Everyone had enough to worry about already. Why should he add to that?

*

Kai enjoyed working in the greenhouse, which was slowly turning green again.

It still amazed him that they could make a plant—a living thing—grow, bloom, and bear fruit with just a handful of dirt and some water. But that wasn't true. Much more went into the task. Growing a garden required knowledge, skill, and a great deal of care. And it was mostly Leah who supplied them. Everyone else, including Kai, just followed her lead.

Kai kept a discreet watch over Leah as he worked.

She was still pale, and her movements were cautious, as if she was afraid to disturb some invisible order. But her eyes shone with energy, and her face lit up with a smile every time a task was finished and another patch of the greenhouse restored. People worked hard just to earn that smile, and Kai was no exception.

Today, Leah lingered by his side.

Kai glanced up from his position on his knees. "I'm almost finished."

He had reused a metal frame from an old canopy bed to serve as support for climbing vines. Now he was struggling to untangle a knotted thread. The plan was to weave the thread top to bottom and then across in a web pattern the vines could climb as they grew.

"Is this okay? I'm thinking to space the threads about a foot apart."

"It's fine." Leah sounded distracted. She wasn't looking at the metal structure. "I want to talk to you."

Kai stood and brushed his hands off on his pants. "Okay."

Leah glanced to the side, and color rose to cheeks. "But not here. I want to talk to you in private. Follow me."

Ana was watching them but quickly turned away.

Kai's chest tightened. He had suspected for a while now that Leah liked him. But he never expected her to act on it. Now anxiety prickled his skin. He had no idea how to respond. The last thing he wanted was to hurt her. But he couldn't lie to her either. She was too smart for that. She would see right through him, and it would only hurt her more.

Leah led him across the hallway to another room. It was a library of sorts. Bookshelves lined two walls and flanked a large window. On the shelves, paper books and framed photos gathered dust. Two faded armchairs faced the window.

Leah turned to Kai. "I trust you, Kai. And I need to ask you something."

His mind was in turmoil. He cared about Leah—just not that way. "Leah, I—"

But she cut him off. "I'm worried about Val."

Kai blinked in surprise—and shame filled him. He was such an idiot. This wasn't about him. Leah wasn't declaring her feelings for him. She wasn't thinking about herself at all. She was thinking about her brother.

"I need your help." She peered into his eyes. "I need someone who will keep an eye on him and have his back in case things go wrong. And stop him from doing anything crazy."

"Did you ask Ana too?" Kai blurted.

"No," Leah said quickly.

Kai already regretted the question. "Sorry, you don't have to tell me."

But she hushed him. "It's okay. You deserve to know." She took a deep breath. "Ana is a complicated person. Do you know this house belongs to her?"

"Yeah. Green mentioned it."

"Did he also tell you what happened to her family?"

"He said her parents were murdered. But she survived."

Pain crossed Leah's face. She walked over to the bookshelf and picked up a framed photo that had been placed face down. She turned it to Kai.

"It wasn't only her parents. It was also her younger sister. She died the same night."

In the photograph, the two sisters stood on the stairs with their arms around each other. The younger one stood a step higher, so they were almost the same height. They wore pretty dresses, and they were laughing. Kai barely recognized Ana. The girl in the photo beamed with happiness, her gaze clear and trusting. He had never seen Ana look like that.

And her little sister... Something tore lose in Kai's chest when he saw the girl's face. She was so young and joyful, it was hard to believe anyone would want to hurt her.

Kai shook himself. "How did Ana survive?"

"She hid in the safe room."

A memory clicked into place. "The same room she hid you in?"

Leah tossed her head angrily. "Yes. It's very secure and practically invisible from the outside." She pointed to one bookshelf. "We're standing in front of it right now."

Kai passed his hand over the decorative paneling of the bookshelf, examining it. There! He found the door frame.

"Very good." Leah pressed a hidden lever, and the door clicked open. She showed him the room inside. It was spacious, with several bunk beds and shelves full of supplies. In the corner was a small bathroom. "We keep it stocked for emergencies."

Kai couldn't help being curious. "So how long did Ana stay in here? How long before the robbers left?"

Leah tensed. "They didn't."

Kai looked at her. "What do you mean?"

Leah met his gaze. "I'm telling you this in confidence." Her voice shook with emotion. "Ana is my best friend and the bravest person I've ever known. I cannot imagine what it was like for her..." She broke off, unable to say it.

But she didn't have to. Kai already knew. "She killed them."

Leah exhaled. "Yes."

"How? She had weapons?" Kai had a vivid memory of Ana's knife at his throat.

"No. She got her knife later," Leah said, as if reading his mind. "Her parents didn't believe in weapons. They opposed all forms of violence."

Kai tried to picture Ana exiting the safe room and facing the gang. Several men, bigger and stronger than her. Ruthless enough to kill a little girl. What could she do to them? And more importantly, what would they do to *her* if they caught her?

"She waited three days. Watched them. Learned their habits." Leah pointed to an array of dark security monitors on one wall. "The house had lots of stuff to sell. They were celebrating. They drank a lot. On the third day, she snuck out and poisoned their drinks."

"She poisoned them?" A chill went through Kai. He thought of Axer tied to the chair, moaning in terror from some drug Ana had given him.

"Ana's parents were pharmacists before they went into research. She grew up watching them mix drugs and print warning labels," Leah continued. "That day, she disregarded all the warnings. She made sure the men who killed her sister died a slow and horrible death." Leah turned away, as if the scene was unfolding in front of her, and walked out of the safe room.

Kai followed. "How do you know all this?"

Leah pushed the bookshelf back in its place. The safe room disappeared. "Because... Val and I saw them right after they died." She shuddered. "We were outside when the smog hit, a terrible one. We knocked on the door, and Ana let us in. The men..." She shook her head. "I will never forget their faces."

Kai had an impulse to put his arms around her. But it felt wrong. So he let them hang uselessly at his sides.

Leah replaced Ana's photo on the shelf, face down, the same way she had found it. Then she resumed her story. "Ana had mixed another batch of drugs for herself. She would have... ended her life that night if we hadn't knocked on her door. She saved us. But we also saved her. Maybe it always works like that."

Brie poked her head in the door, startling them both. "Leah? Here you are! We got the sprinkler to work again!"

Leah gave a weak smile. "I'll be there in a second, okay?"

Brie's gaze went from Leah to Kai, then back to Leah. A frown appeared on her small face. "Okay. Sure." And she was gone.

Leah turned to Kai, her tone more urgent now. "The thing is, I *can't* ask Ana. Ana loves Val. I know she does. But she loves *me* more. She loves me like she did her little sister." Something caught in Leah's voice. "That's why I can't trust her. Not when Val is involved. I know she'll choose me over him. It'll kill her. But that's what she'll do." Leah peered into his face. "That's why I'm asking *you.* Promise me that you'll stop Val if he tries to do anything stupid!"

"Don't worry. Val won't do anything stupid," Kai tried to reassure her.

But Leah only tossed her head impatiently. "Come on, Kai. I know about the drug Ana gave me. And I know it was the last dose. Which means my brother will do anything to get more of it."

Kai's memory yanked him back in time. He saw Leah's body on the ground, her eyes closed and her chest too still, and fear gripped him. "And we will! We'll get that drug for you."

He wondered if Leah knew about the artificial heart. But whether she did or not, he wasn't going to bring it up.

Leah smiled. "Don't get me wrong. I want my heart to keep beating." Her expression hardened. "But not if the price is too high. Do you understand?"

Kai wanted to protest that she didn't have to worry about that. But something about her expression stopped him. "I understand."

Leah's shoulders relaxed a little. "Val still thinks I'm a little girl, and he has to take care of me. But I'm not. I'm stronger than he thinks." Affection warmed her voice. "My brother is a good man. He feels responsible for all of us and wants to protect us. But he's not indestructible either. And I don't want anything to happen to him because of *me*."

"I'll watch his back," Kai said solemnly. "You have my word."

"Thank you." Leah smiled and touched his hand, her fingers cold as ice. "I knew I could count on you." Then she turned and left the library, moving as lightly and soundlessly as a ghost.

24
KAI

FROM THEN ON, Kai watched Val and waited. Whatever Val was planning, he couldn't delay it for long. Every day without the drug put Leah's life at risk. Val had no choice. He had to act.

Normally, that would mean closed-door meetings with Zip, Ana, and a few others, depending on the job. In these meetings, Val and his team fleshed out the details of the mission and decided the security measures to be taken at home while the team was away, since security was still a priority after Slayer's attack. Then Val would share the final plan with the entire group, although usually on a need-to-know basis, to minimize the risks.

Kai kept a close eye for such meetings, but none took place. On the contrary, Val kept to himself and hardly spoke to anybody. Which told Kai that whatever scheme Leah's brother was devising to secure more heart medication for his sister—he intended to carry it out alone. Most likely at night, when he only had to get past whoever's turn it was to stand guard, and everyone else was asleep.

When, at dinner, Val got up from the long table and walked out of the kitchen, Kai barely noticed. He hadn't slept all night, waiting for Val to make his move—all in vain—and had spent most of the day helping Marco build new bunk beds for the Rats, while racing downstairs any chance he got to check on Val. Now he was nearly dozing off over his plate of off-color spaghetti and the only person at the table not complaining about it.

"Nice colors, Ivy," Karim teased.

"She's an artist," Riko agreed.

"It looks like alien puke!" Max pitched in.

The food printer had glitched again, and the spaghetti sauce came out purple instead of red and smelling of burnt rubber. Since Ivy was in charge of dinner, the group was letting her hear it.

"Then don't eat it!" she snapped. "Who's forcing you?"

Kai glanced at Val's untouched pasta and clean fork—and it finally registered. Val got away!

He sprang to his feet and rushed out of the kitchen.

Ivy's curse and the group's laughter followed him. They took his abrupt exit for a joke.

But Kai raced to the front door, cursing himself for not paying better attention. Val had outsmarted him. He must have realized Kai was keeping tabs on him and chosen a perfect time to lose his shadow. Kai wanted to punch himself.

Hans sat cross-legged in the foyer, fiddling with a circuit board. He was the guard.

"Val gone out just now?" Kai demanded.

Startled, Hans nearly snapped the board in half. He threw an uncertain glance at the door. "Er..."

"Got it. Thanks." Kai turned the lock and slammed outside.

Smog drifted down the street. He turned from left to right, squinting against the dust and the fading daylight. "Damn it, Val. Which way did you go?"

He just barely made out a familiar silhouette wearing a large backpack two blocks away on the right. The man was just turning the corner. A moment later, and Kai would have lost him.

Kai sprinted in that direction.

"Val, wait up!" He caught up to him and blocked his way. "Where are you off to?"

Val glared at him. "I don't have time for this. Get out of my way."

Kai didn't budge. "Can't."

The red-haired man gritted his teeth. "I don't know what my sister told you. But I'm warning you. You *can't* stop me, so don't even try." He squared his shoulders and took a step forward, as if to plow his way through Kai's body.

"I won't stop you," Kai said. "But I'm going with you."

Guilt slashed through him as soon as he spoke the words. This wasn't exactly what he had promised Leah.

Even so, Val tried to push past him. "Like hell, you are."

But Kai grabbed his arm, anger and impatience flaring in his gut. "Listen! You won't get rid of me. So we can argue and waste time—or we can *help Leah.* Which one is it going to be?"

Val yanked his arm from Kai's grasp. He leveled his fierce gaze at Kai. "Fine," he spit out. "But you do what I tell you, no questions asked. And if anything goes wrong—you're on your own. Understand?"

Kai almost smiled. "Loud and clear."

Val pulled out his face mask. "You'll need—"

Kai slipped on his own mask. He had learned to keep it on him at all times. The mask muffled his voice when he spoke. "Now do you want to tell me where we're going?"

But Val only stepped around him and started walking. "No."

Kai fell in step with him, and they walked in silence, dusk settling around them.

They followed the familiar street to its dead end, then turned into a narrow alley, cutting under one overpass, then another. Soon they were in another sector of the megacity, one Kai had never been to before.

A jolt went through him, and even before he knew what he was doing, he was scanning the masked faces of people who passed him in the street, searching for her.

Emily.

Was she here? What if he ran into her right now? What would he say to her?

But he pushed the thoughts away.

Next to him, Val walked with his gaze fixed straight ahead, never turning his head, never hesitating, as if he had travelled this path many times and knew it by heart.

It was evening by the time they stopped at the edge of a huge parking lot. The lot was empty except for a few battered cars standing at odd angles under the only remaining street light. The only sound was a rustle of plastic trash rolling in the wind across the cracked asphalt.

At first, Kai thought the building ahead was another abandoned factory. The structure was massive and had seen better days. But it was the wrong shape. Instead of one solid block, it looked like a dozen different buildings had been fitted together in a haphazard 3D puzzle and linked by a web of skywalks. The only thing the pieces had in common were dark, smog-coated windows staring into the night like empty eye sockets.

"What is this place?" Kai asked.

Val's voice was grim. "Bad news." Still, he limped doggedly across the parking lot.

A row of ticket booths lined the exit from the lot. All were dark and empty. One had been smashed and lay on its side, torn cables sticking out of the square floor.

A shadow detached itself from the nearest booth, forming a silhouette of a tall woman in a fitted jacket and pants.

"Stay here," Val told Kai, before heading in the woman's direction.

Curiosity drew him a few steps closer.

Val approached the booth and stood with his back to Kai, as if to block his view of the woman or perhaps her view of him. But she suddenly stepped around him.

Kai caught sight of heavily made-up eyes over a face mask and a strand of long, blond hair poking from under her hood. The woman looked straight at him with shrewd eyes.

"Who's your friend?" she asked loud enough for Kai to hear.

Val glanced over his shoulder, frowning. Turning back to the woman, he reached into his pocket, pulled out a small object, and offered it to her. He spoke to her in a low, urgent voice Kai couldn't hear.

The woman hesitated, glancing at Kai once more, her eyes narrowing. Then her fingers closed around Val's offering—which could only be a roll of cash—while she passed him another, even smaller object.

Val nodded to her, and the woman withdrew, melting into the shadow of the booth.

The transaction was over.

Val looked back over his shoulder and motioned to Kai. *Let's go.* He started walking without waiting for him, heading straight for the dark, massive building.

"What did you get?" Kai asked, catching up to him.

Without a word, Val extended his hand. A small bunch of keys lay in his open palm.

Kai frowned. "And how did *she* get them?"

Val stuck the keys back in his pocket. "She used to work here."

Doing what? Kai still didn't know what the place was. He thought of the woman's calculating eyes. "And... you trust her?"

"I don't," Val snapped, annoyed. "So how about you

stop talking, and we do what we're here to do and get out?"

They reached the end of the parking lot and turned into a driveway that rounded the building. It brought them to a wide entrance. Shattered sliding doors lead into a dark and silent interior. *Emergency*, read a faded sign above the doors.

So the place used to be a hospital. And a huge one.

Kai's shoulders relaxed. At least the location made sense. Hospitals used drugs.

Val headed inside, and Kai followed.

Even through his mask, a thick odor of blood, urine, and chemicals hit him when he entered, turning his stomach.

Val paused in the dark lobby, listening. When no sound came from the hallway ahead, he pulled out a small flashlight. The bright beam caught a dark red stain on the floor. He shaded the light with his hand. "Come on. It's this way."

Kai expected to turn into one of the examination rooms that lay on both sides of the hallway, some doors torn off the hinges, others broken in, revealing upturned beds, ransacked cabinets, and smashed electronic equipment inside. But Val led him to a staircase at the other end.

They climbed five flights of stairs splattered with more dark stains and littered with syringes, their steps echoing in the silence. The entire building appeared to be deserted. And Kai wasn't surprised. Nobody in the sectors could afford hospitals.

The hallway they entered was narrower than the one on the first floor. Kai peered into the rooms they passed.

They looked more like a research lab than a hospital wing. Not like Neen's lab, though. There were no models of prosthetic limbs here, no circuit boards, no 3D printers. Instead, glass containers of all shapes and sizes lined the shelves above wide counters equipped with sinks, small microwaves, and hooded work stations. A chemical lab of some sort, less damaged than the rooms downstairs. Although some cabinets gaped open, with broken glass and plastic gloves strewn all over the counters and the floor underneath them.

Without stopping, Val pulled out the keys and checked them under his flashlight. He aimed the light at each room number as he passed them.

Kai swallowed behind his mask. Did Val plan to actually *make* the drug for Leah? Was this what the labs were used for when the hospital was still open—to make drugs for the patients?

Key in hand, Val turned into the lab at the end of the hallway. But instead of stopping at one of the counters, he continued toward the back of the room.

The last aisle was wider than the other aisles, and asymmetrical. It had a working counter and overhead cabinets on one side. But the opposite side—the back wall—held a row of tall refrigerators, their doors left half open.

Kai peered inside one, but the dark shelves looked empty. Somebody else had already cleaned them out of whatever had been stored inside. More broken glass crunched under his feet.

Kai's heart sank. What if they were too late and all the drugs were gone?

But Val kept going, stopping only when he reached an indistinct door at the very end of the room.

He unlocked it with fumbling fingers and nearly ran inside, his limp momentarily gone.

Kai expected simple shelves, like in a storage closet. But instead, tall, steel cabinets were built into the two opposite walls. Each held a dozen deep drawers. Val turned to the drawers on the right with eager, hopeful eyes.

He yanked on the first drawer. But it was locked.

Kai stopped in the doorway. The storage room was too small for two people. "I can hold the flashlight," he offered.

"Yeah. Okay." Val handed him the flashlight. "Keep it on my hands, will you?" He sounded almost cheerful. As soon as he had the light, he found the proper key and unlocked the first drawer.

But Kai felt a stab of apprehension. The lab suddenly reminded him of the Training Center. He thought he heard the low hum of electronics coming from the walls. But how could that be? The building was abandoned. Where would the power come from?

And there was something else...

Val got the first drawer open and rummaged inside it. Not finding what he wanted, he pushed it closed again and moved to the next drawer.

Kai turned off the flashlight.

"Hey," Val protested, and Kai quickly turned the light back on. But now he was sure. Unlike the other labs—unlike the rest of the building—this lab *wasn't* entirely dark. Faint light emanated from the ceiling. But *why?*

Kai's skin crawled. "We should hurry up," he said, trying to sound casual.

Val made a sound of impatience. Apparently, the second drawer didn't have what he needed either. He slammed it shut and moved on to the third one. He fumbled with the key again.

"Yeah!" he boomed, pulling out a handful of boxes from the open drawer. He shrugged off his backpack and started stuffing the boxes into it. He grinned widely. "We're good. We won't run out again. We're good."

Kai was about to smile back—when bright light and piercing sound exploded around him.

The flashlight flew from his hand, and he stumbled back, disoriented. The ceiling lights flashed on and off, blinding him. The siren drilled into his skull with a maddening intensity. The floor vibrated under his prosthetic feet, and some heavy object slammed down.

What was happening?

Kai spun around, the flashing lights slicing the space around him. He bumped into the counter, turned back. He tore the mask off his face. "Val?" he yelled over the noise. "Val? Come on! We've got to get out of here!"

Then he saw Val—and froze.

Thick metal bars blocked the doorway to the storage room.

Val was trapped inside.

25
KAI

WITH THE BLASTING SIREN and flashing lights beating down on him like vicious fists, Kai rushed toward the storage room. He gripped the metal bars and pulled on them. But they didn't budge.

The storage room had become a cage.

Inside it, Val stood shell-shocked, his eyes wide and his breathing ragged.

Then he blinked and shook himself. His gaze dropped to the backpack he was clutching, now filled with the narrow boxes from the drawer, and his face hardened with determination. He wasn't going anywhere, and he knew it. But Leah could still get the drugs she needed. She *had* to get them. Even if he never made it.

Kai read all of this in Val's face, and fear stabbed him.

No. He couldn't leave Val behind. He had given Leah his word.

"Hold on." Kai spun around, spotted a tall metal stool under the counter. He fetched it. It was heavy. *Good.* "Stand back!" He swung the stool at the bars of the cage as hard as he could.

Metal slammed against metal with such force that Kai felt the vibrations in his teeth.

Two legs of the stool bent from the impact. But the bars of the cage remained intact.

Val rammed the backpack in between the metal bars. The pack barely fit, but he worked it through the opening. "Take it!" he screamed at Kai over the siren. "Take it and get out!"

Kai gritted his teeth. He couldn't leave. Not without Val.

He scanned the doorway to the storage room. Then aimed at the wall left of it and swung the stool again.

The wall cracked but Kai felt the familiar impact in his arms. There was metal underneath the cement. He threw the stool down. It wasn't strong enough.

"What are you doing? There's no time!" Val screamed, shaking the backpack outside the bars. "Take it and get out! Get the hell out of here! *Go!"* He awkwardly threw the pack at Kai.

Kai leapt forward and caught it before it fell.

He glanced down at his feet, and hope surged in his chest. His prostheses! They were stronger than the stool.

He set the backpack on the counter and eyed the metal bars, planning his move. He had barely three yards of space to work with, not enough to gain speed. And there was a good chance that he'd break both legs. But he had to try.

Inside the cage, Val glared at him, shaking his head. "No! Don't be stupid! Get out!" But he reflexively stepped back.

Kai ran two steps and launched himself upward.

Midair, he twisted sideways, drawing his knees to his chest—and then straightened his legs, releasing the kick.

Pain shot through him, sharp and electric, as his prostheses connected with the metal bars—and he fell, elbow first, on the hard floor.

He turned his head to the cage and scanned the metal bars.

Two were bent! It had worked!

Inside the cage, Val staggered and slid to the floor, pawing at the drawers as he went, a look of confusion on his face.

"Val?" Kai tried to get up, but the room swam around him, his head suddenly heavy and a bitter, chemical taste in his mouth.

Something hissed in between the relentless peaks of the siren...

Gas!

With desperate urgency, Kai gripped the metal bars, trying to pull himself up.

What had he done? He should have listened to Val. Leah needed the drugs!

But his legs folded under him, his lungs straining for air, and the room around him already fading away.

Two seconds later, his head hit the floor, and he passed out.

*

When Kai came to, his vision was blurry and there was a ringing in his ears. But the flashing lights and blaring siren were gone. He was no longer lying on the floor but sitting up, his back and arms supported, his legs stretched in front of him. An armchair?

Kai blinked to refocus his eyes—and recoiled.

Peter Falcon's cold eyes studied him.

His former Sponsor sat across a low table from him in another armchair, his legs casually crossed. A panoramic view of the megacity stretched behind him, the drifting smog suggesting a real window. A large executive desk stood off to the side.

They were in... an office. But how?

Cold sweat broke over Kai. "Where's Val?" he rasped, his mouth and throat parched and his thoughts still sluggish.

A groan answered him. Kai turned to his other side.

Val half lay in an armchair next to him, his eyes still

closed, and his chest rising and falling slowly. He groaned again, still unconscious.

Kai scanned the room for security guards but saw none.

"You have no reason to be concerned," Falcon said. "I intend you and your friend no harm." He caught the wary look on Kai's face and added, "My men are searching for someone. Had I known they might run into you, I would have instructed them to treat you with more consideration. Naturally, you are *not* the person we are after. However," Falcon reached down and lifted Val's backpack onto the table, "I must admit that I *am* curious to hear an explanation. Care to enlighten me?"

Before Kai could answer, Val stirred, and his eyes popped open. At the sight of Falcon, he blinked rapidly and started to rise. "What...? How did I...? What is this?"

Kai reached out and grabbed Val's arm, pulling him back down. "Val! It's me. It's okay. You're okay. Sit down."

Val dropped back onto the chair, but he glared at Falcon with unmasked hostility.

Falcon showed no sign of alarm or unease. He regarded Val coolly for a moment, then turned his attention back to Kai. "By the way, it may interest you to know that your prostheses are not seriously damaged."

Kai stiffened at the memory of the kick and the sharp pain that followed it, his gaze automatically sliding down to his outstretched legs.

"I took the liberty of running a quick diagnostic," Falcon continued. "Only a minor defect in one circuit. Nothing you'll miss. You were lucky, considering what you attempted."

Despite himself, Kai breathed with relief. What would he do if his prostheses *were* seriously damaged? He was suddenly angry with himself and with Falcon. "What was I supposed to do? He was trapped! I couldn't just leave him there!"

Next to him, Val jumped to his feet. "That's exactly what you should have done! I told you to leave me and get out!" His eyes fell on the backpack on the low table, then cut to the closed door, as if he might snatch the pack and make a run for it. But he took one limping step and stopped. Then just stood there, his shoulders slumped and a look of bitter defeat on his face. "And now it's all over," he muttered.

Falcon picked up the backpack and retrieved one box. He opened it and examined the drug-filled syringe. He clearly knew what it was. "An effective emergency measure. But a very short-term solution." He replaced the drug in the backpack and moved the pack out of sight. Then he addressed Val, "Is there a big market for it in the sectors?"

"It wasn't for sale," Val growled. Then he lowered his head and added, "It was for my sister."

"I see." No emotion registered on Falcon's face. He considered the information for a moment. Then leaned forward and tapped the control panel on the table. The surface split open, and a hidden tray appeared, bearing a square case. Falcon picked it up.

Val frowned with suspicion. "What is it?"

But Kai's pulse quickened, his eyes fixed on the case in his Sponsor's hands. Could it be—?

With the case resting in one open palm, Falcon touched the top with his other hand. The case briefly lit up and then sprang open, the sides folding themselves down to a flat base, and revealing the object inside, now on full display.

A sleek artificial heart.

Val sucked in his breath. "Is that—?"

"Titan SI 200." Pride rang in Falcon's voice. "Self-powered and fully implantable, it comes in several standard sizes to match the person's anatomy, and the outer coating is bio-printed from the patient's own tissue, which eliminates the risk of immune rejection. A state-of-the-art self-monitoring system lets it adapt to any foreseeable conditions. Far beyond restoring cardiovascular health, Titan endows its recipient with a physical endurance on par with the best trained athletes."

The flashy TV ad for replacement organs replayed in Kai's head.

"'Live two hundred years in perfect health'," Val recited in a choked voice, as if he and Kai were tuned to the same channel. "'Only from 3D Electronics'."

Falcon nodded. "Naturally, I could be accused of being biased, since it was developed by my own research team. But evidence from extensive testing supports my view. Titan is by far the most powerful and reliable artificial heart ever produced. In fact, it is superior even to the healthiest biological heart." He extended his hand, offering the device to Kai. "Please."

Kai hesitated.

"Go ahead," Falcon encouraged. "You can't break it."

Kai picked up the heart and turned it in his fingers. It was uncanny how much the device resembled a real heart—or what Kai knew about them from discount online courses. Only the material felt strange against Kai's skin, unlike anything he had ever touched. But then he'd never held a real heart either.

Kai stared at the heart—and imagined it coming to life in his hands, a contraction rippling through the four chambers, from one side to the other.

The heart was beating.

He blinked—and the vision was gone. The heart was perfectly still and cool to the touch. Lifeless.

"It's not beating," he blurted out.

Falcon smiled. "It doesn't need to beat yet. There's no blood to pump, no person to keep alive. But I can assure you that once it's implanted and activated, it will beat for a very long time." He placed the folded box on the table and leaned back in his chair.

Kai's thoughts went to Leah, and for a moment, a strange sensation gripped him.

It was Leah's heart he was holding—cold and still and without life.

A mix of emotions ripped through him, and he hurriedly put the heart back on the table.

"Impressive, is it not?" Falcon watched him closely. "It will make heart disease a thing of the past. But, of course, restoring healthy function is just the beginning." The Sponsor's voice rang with conviction. "Titan will usher a completely new era—one in which the human species will finally overcome its biological limitations and take control of its evolution."

Val moved to the table and picked up the heart. "How much... does it cost?"

A memory sprang to Kai's mind. Green scrolling through the product description of the artificial heart on his computer, his expression grim. *No one can afford to* buy *it. But they can pay per month.* Artificial organs—for lease. Kai felt the old horror.

Falcon studied Val for a moment. Then he said, "In this case—nothing."

Val's face darkened. "Nothing, huh?" He gripped the heart with both hands, as if he wanted to smash it.

Kai got to his feet. "Val. Take it easy."

"Your sister needs it. Does she not?" Falcon held Val's gaze. "So I suggest you do not delay. A hovercraft can pick her up tomorrow morning. My medical staff will take care of the rest. She will go home with a new heart in three days' time."

Blood drained from Val's face and he stumbled, the precious device nearly slipping from his shaking fingers. "You're... serious?" he breathed, staring at Falcon with wide eyes. "You would... do that?"

Falcon waved his hand dismissively. "Consider it a gift."

Val swallowed. "But... why? You know we can't pay you back. You'll be... losing money."

Falcon's eyes moved to Kai's face, as if to say that his reply to Val also referred to him.

Kai tensed. He thought of the last day of the Race, of throwing his chance at victory to stop Slayer and help Venus win. How much had that cost Falcon? And what if he decided to punish Kai for it now?

"It's true that I will lose a considerable amount of money, and it is definitely not my habit to do so," Falcon explained, his eyes still on Kai. "But in this case, I'm willing to make an exception—because I'm curious."

"Curious about what?" Kai asked.

"To see what the recipient of my gift will do with it," Falcon said simply. "How they will use it. What they will accomplish."

Kai knew he should keep his mouth shut, but he couldn't help it. "What if... you're disappointed?"

Val threw him a sharp look, but he ignored it.

"Well, that's always the risk. But I very much doubt that I will be," Falcon said. "I realize it takes time to see things clearly. To get used to the new power, the new possibilities. But such clarity will come. And when it does, and it spreads and grows, it will crush the fear and prejudice that still rule over our society."

"What fear and prejudice?" Val asked, an intense, eager look on his face. Either Falcon's speech or his promised gift had erased his distrust already.

"Let me show you something." Falcon tapped his wrist, where a faint display glowed against his skin, and a large hologram screen appeared in front of them. Falcon gestured for them to sit back down. "And then you are free to go."

Kai and Val exchanged a look and took their seats.

Val hesitated, then replaced the artificial heart on the flat tray. Instantly, the walls folded themselves around it, until the device vanished inside the box.

An image of an empty alley, shot from a drone high above, filled the projected screen.

"I should warn you," Falcon said. "I found this footage very disturbing, and I suspect you will as well."

The video came to life, the frame shifting along the alley, the camera zooming in—and Kai shuddered in shock.

A man in an insect-print suit—the man from the cage race!—lay in a puddle of blood, his arms splayed to the sides and his eyes staring. Dead.

No—worse than dead. Because the man's chest was a rugged, gaping hole.

Someone had ripped out his heart.

26
KAI

KAI STARED at the torn and bloodied chest of the dead man in the hologram, a gaping cavity where his heart used to be, unable to comprehend what he was seeing.

The man's frantic, desperate face rose in his memory, after he had bet on Kai at the cage race and lost it all. *You've killed me. I'm a dead man.* As if he had already known someone was after him, and had hoped to ward them off with his winnings...

Val stomped forward, interrupting Kai's thoughts. "Who did this?" he demanded through clenched teeth. His fists hung like two hammers at his sides, ready to pound.

"Good question." Falcon tapped his wrist, and the holographic display split into a dozen screens.

The video of the dead man in the alley continued to play in the center, already looping in time. The rest of the screens showed the streets and apartment buildings nearby, each from a different angle, but all shot from above.

Kai scanned the screens, unease gnawing at him. Leah was getting a new heart. He should be happy. But Falcon was showing them the videos for a reason. Kai didn't trust him.

"Unfortunately, none of the security drones captured the thief in the act," Falcon said.

"You mean, the *murderer?"* Kai corrected.

Falcon's cold eyes narrowed a fraction. "Actually, in this case, the law of the Alliance recognizes *theft* as the more severe crime, and one punished with a harsher sentence. Biomedical patent violation is a threat to the whole society." A hard edge had crept into his voice, but he quickly caught himself and continued in a calm voice. "But, of course, to the victim, the difference between theft and murder is purely semantic, since the consequence is the same."

Unless he was already dead.

And suddenly, it all fell into place.

The man in the insect suit didn't own the artificial heart in his chest—he leased it. He looked wealthy, but appearances could be deceiving. In reality, for whatever reason, he may have been flat broke. What happened if you leased a computer and couldn't make a payment? The computer got taken away. No wonder the man was desperate. He knew he was about to die.

But who really killed him?

Was it the thief who took his heart? Or was it Falcon's team, sent to repossess the company's property?

Kai's gaze snapped to Falcon, the suspicion burning in his gut.

Falcon met his gaze, his face as inscrutable as if it was carved from stone. "You have questions."

But it was Val who spoke up. "Yeah, I do." The red-haired man had been studying the holographic display with intense focus, as if his own life depended on it. "How come the video of the dead man is so short?" he demanded. "Where's the rest of it? Where's the *before?"*

Falcon nodded appreciatively. "Indeed. It looks like someone interfered with the drone's transmission. The video files that you refer to were never recorded on the server."

Val stared at him. "You mean the guy who did this

also hacked the drone?"

"I doubt it was one man," Falcon replied. Then, seeing confusion on Val's face, he elaborated. "You must know there are people who oppose biomedical technology, some of them very powerful. They see it as an aberration that will corrupt humanity and destroy the natural order of things, and they believe it's their duty to stop it by any means and at any cost."

Kai tensed. *The Collectors.*

"The natural order, huh?" Val scowled. "Like my sister almost dying when she was ten?"

Falcon nodded. "I find it hard to comprehend as well. The same people deny that self-improvement is a basic human drive and our highest aspiration. They would rather preserve the status quo, no matter how cruel and unjust, than to overcome their fear and prejudice. They distrust and abhor all biotechnology, and want everyone else to distrust and abhor it too."

Kai glanced at Val. Leah's brother listened hungrily, nodding in agreement, the last trace of hostility toward their host gone. Falcon had gained a follower.

Kai wished he could feel the same conviction, but his mind was in turmoil and wouldn't settle.

He thought of Olympia Livingstone in her airborne mansion, coldly refusing to save Leah's life, even when Kai begged her for help. *Money is not a concern. It's a matter of principle.* And now Falcon was offering Leah a new heart, unasked.

Kai didn't know what to make of it. His mind was still spinning, churning the information, unable to decide. But his gut told him not to trust Falcon. There was more to the story. The heart wasn't really a gift. Falcon expected something in return. If not now, then later.

But what? And more importantly... what happened if they couldn't deliver it?

Kai had an impulse to grab Val's arm and pull him

from the room and away from Falcon.

But Val would never leave. He couldn't turn his back on Falcon's offer, no matter what strings came attached with it. And neither could Kai.

Val glared at the center screen, where the silent footage of the dead man with his ripped chest played on a continuous loop. "Whoever did this," he said through clenched teeth. "I don't care how powerful they are. They can't get away with it. We have to find them and make them pay."

Kai froze, looking at his Sponsor. This was it. They would learn the true price of Leah's heart.

Falcon rose to his feet. "Yes, we do. And we will." He walked toward Val. "But we have to be cautious. Our enemies are shrewd. A loud search would only alert them."

We. Our. Kai watched the two men, frowning.

"So what, we just sit around and do nothing?" Val demanded. "We let them attack someone else? Rip out another heart?"

"No." Falcon put his hand on Val's shoulder. "We stay vigilant. We keep our eyes open. So when they make their next move, we'll be ready."

Val nodded and started to turn, but Falcon's fingers dug into his arm, staying him. "But I need that man alive. Do you understand?"

Val straightened. "I understand."

Falcon's hand dropped from Val's arm. "Good. My men will drop you off wherever you want and wait for you there tomorrow morning. Make sure your sister is ready at eight a.m. We do not allow visitors, so you won't be able to visit her until she's discharged. But I assure you, she will receive the highest quality of care."

Val swallowed. "She'll be ready. Thank you." He took a step toward the door.

Falcon glanced at Val's leg. "We should take care of your leg, too, some time."

"I..." Val's voice caught in his throat.

Falcon raised his hand, signaling that there was no need to thank him. "I've held you long enough."

Val bowed his head and walked out of the office. Kai started after him when an incoming message flashed on the holographic screen.

Kai caught a glimpse of the caller before Falcon flicked his wrist and the hologram blinked out.

Slayer.

Adrenaline surged through Kai, all his suspicions renewed. What was that about? He stopped, turning back to Falcon.

"I lost you money in the Race." A challenge more than an apology.

No emotion showed on Falcon's face. "I thought you knew by now that to me, money is merely a means to an end. I also don't believe in dwelling on the past. I find it more productive to look to the future and... consider the bigger picture."

"I'll keep that in mind." Kai hesitated, wanting to ask about Slayer. But he couldn't risk it. He turned and followed Val out the door.

Val and two security guards waited for him in the hallway. Val gave him a questioning look, but Kai was careful to keep his expression blank. "Sorry. Let's go."

What would Val do if he knew Falcon was talking to Slayer right now? Kai pushed the question away. He didn't want to find out.

They rode Falcon's hovercraft in silence. It dropped them off just two blocks away from Ana's house, and they arranged for Leah to be picked up from the same location the next morning.

When the hovercraft left, Val grabbed Kai's arm. "Listen. Let me do the talking. Okay? Leah doesn't need to know everything. Especially not about the... dead man." His jaw clenched tight.

"Fine by me." Kai wasn't eager to tell Leah how he had let her brother walk right into a trap.

Leah would live, he told himself. She would get a new heart. It was more than he had hoped for.

But his skin still crawled with unease.

Falcon hadn't told them the whole truth. Kai knew that much. But what had he left out?

Only minutes later, they entered the house and faced Leah. Kai stood next to Val when he shared the good news with his sister. The rest of the group had gathered around them, listening intently.

Leah paled and shook her head. "I don't understand. We can't pay for it. How did you get it? What did you have to do?" She scanned her brother's body as if she expected a missing limb or worse. "Tell me the truth."

Val had an answer ready. "Nothing. I didn't have to do anything, Leah. I swear it." His eyes moved to Kai. "We have Sand Runner to thank for it. The gift is from his Sponsor. He runs 3D Electronics. They make the hearts. They can afford to give one away."

Kai blinked, taken aback. What happened to Val doing all the talking?

He caught Ana's gaze. She stared at him hard, her eyes brimming with tears.

He swallowed and nodded. "Yeah. That's right. He's my Sponsor. *Was.*"

Leah frowned, still unconvinced. "But why would he help *me?* He's never even met me. What does he care what happens to me?"

Kai's own doubts and suspicions pressed in, burning in his gut. But now wasn't the time to share them. He couldn't do it to Leah, to Val, to any of them. Still, he couldn't lie either. "He doesn't," he blurted out. "Not really."

Val's face twisted, and he glared at Kai. But Leah's shoulders relaxed a notch. "Then why give me the heart?"

"Because he's a strange guy," Kai said cautiously. "And he's curious."

Leah cocked her head, her eyes shining with intelligence. "Curious?"

Kai hesitated. But he couldn't back out now. "Curious to see what you'll do with your life, what you'll accomplish with his gift," he explained, conscious of how cold and callous his explanation sounded.

Around him, the group shifted in disapproval, people murmuring in low voices and exchanging dark looks.

But Leah only laughed, color creeping into her pale cheeks. "I see. Your Sponsor *is* strange. I'll do my best not to waste his gift!"

Val exhaled with relief, then grasped his sister's hand in both of his. "So you'll do it?"

"Yes, Val. I'll do it," Leah said. "If that strange man wants to give me a new heart, I'll take it."

The group cheered and pushed closer, engulfing the siblings in a group hug.

Without thinking, Kai stepped out of the way, and immediately felt guilty. What was wrong with him? Leah would live! He should be grateful. He should be celebrating with the others.

But how could he trust Falcon?

Emily never did.

And despite everything, Kai still trusted her.

27
EMILY

EMILY WALKED BRISKLY down a narrow street, her hood low over her eyes and the tails of her long coat trailing behind her. She had her backpack with her—she never went anywhere without it. Inside it was her tablet and Victor's artificial heart, wrapped in Kai's jacket, together with some provisions she had bought for dinner. Dusk was falling, and the air was chilly but clear.

The street ahead sloped upward until it became a bridge over an old, empty expressway. Somewhere nearby, a familiar music echoed between the cement walls of the buildings.

A small crowd of sector dwellers had gathered in the middle of the bridge, their faces all turned to the right, in the direction of the business district, eyes fixed on a large holographic screen projected there. An audience watching a show. Blocking Emily's way.

She hesitated. But a detour would take her too much out of her way. She kept walking.

A man in a hooded jacket glanced over his shoulder at her when she approached. She nodded to him in greeting, and he nodded in return, before turning his attention back to the screen. A painted face glared at her from his hood, eyes wild and the mouth open in a scream.

The music soared, and Emily's gaze swung past the crowd to the screen, her heart already pounding as painful memories rushed through her mind.

Kai.

In the hologram, Meghan Moore and her new male co-host sat side by side in the studio. "That's right! Your wait is almost over," Meghan was nearly shouting, her lips stretched in a manic smile. "The Eleventh Global No Limits Race starts in three weeks—and I guarantee you, it will be more spectacular than anything you can imagine!"

A mosaic of past Runners filled the screen, and Emily held her breath, half hoping and half dreading catching a glimpse of Kai among them.

But a moment later, the mosaic exploded, the images flying in all directions, followed by a violent burst of flames.

The flames stretched into a line—the start line of the race—and the camera panned alongside it as one Runner after another stepped up to it. Each one had two prosthetic legs and one prosthetic arm. Three Runners were women.

The crowd shifted in alarm and displeasure, heads turning and voices murmuring.

Emily frowned. Were they really so shocked by the female Runners? But then several people spun around and pushed past her, hurrying away.

A drone had appeared over the bridge and was moving in their direction.

The rest of the crowd quickly dispersed, but Emily stood still for a moment longer, deciding.

She wasn't wearing her face mask. It would be smarter to keep her back to the drone, like everyone else.

But recklessness surged through her. Why should she be cautious? What difference did it make?

She lifted her chin and headed down the bridge, straight for the drone.

It hovered in the air above her as she passed it, and she could feel the camera eye trained on her. But it didn't follow her.

She let out the breath she'd been holding. She wasn't sure she could've outrun the drone if it had followed her. She wasn't sure she had the energy to run at all.

*

Later that night, in the apartment, she sat with her tablet in an old armchair, her legs folded under her and covered with a faded blanket that did her absolutely no good. It was a corner apartment in an old building, and the wind howled and slammed against two walls, the chilly air whistling as it pushed inside through the cracks around the buckling windows. Every time a draft cut through the room, she shivered.

She had been here less than a week, after leaving Xander's place, but already the cold had seeped deep into her bones. The electricity came and went, but none of the heaters worked. When she took a shower, the water was like an icy whip. She had to clench her jaw to keep her teeth from rattling. At night, she slept under a pile of blankets and coats she found in the apartment's only closet. But no matter what she did, she couldn't get warm.

She should have turned around and left the first time the power went out, found another place to stay, warmer and more welcoming. But the truth was, she hardly cared anymore.

She was losing heart.

She had always thought that if she could only get access to Falcon's database, if she could only get the proof she needed, everything else would fall into place. She would pass the information on to the others, spread it as widely as possible, and they would heed her warning and act. Together, they would stop the cruel, unnecessary deaths. After all, the artificial hearts weren't that expensive to produce. Where did the horrendous price come from? There had to be a way for 3D Electronics to make the hearts available to those who needed them and still make a profit. And if not, the device could be hacked and the kill switch blocked somehow, no matter what Neen stubbornly believed.

But now, after witnessing two deaths first hand and learning just how utterly helpless she was to prevent them, to do anything for Falcon's victims at all, Emily was gripped by bitter doubts. She had risked everything to get access to the database, and now that the information was under her fingertips, what had she done with it? What had she accomplished?

Other than pushing away the one person she most cared about in the world.

Kai's face rose in her memory, and her chest tightened.

If she found him right now and tried to explain, would he listen? Would he understand? Or would he turn his back on her and walk away? It had been months since she'd left, without ever explaining why. She couldn't blame him if he had given up on her and moved on, maybe even found someone else.

Emily put the tablet away and stretched, her muscles stiff and joints aching from the cold. She paced the small room. Her backpack lay in the far corner, so as not interfere with her wireless. She picked it up and took out the artificial heart.

She turned it in her palms, examining it for the hundredth time. "How do you turn it off, Falcon?" she muttered in frustration. "I know you can. I've seen it. But *how* does it work?"

She sighed and shook her head. She had hoped Neen would solve the puzzle. But the Print Maker was adamant the heart had no off-switch, and without her expertise, Emily was stuck.

She slipped the heart back in the backpack, inside the protective cocoon of Kai's jacket, and picked up the tablet again.

She scrolled through the open folder, scanning the files. Each file was a patient late on their lease, as of today. She stared at the first file, willing herself to open it, but unable to do it, helplessness choking her.

It would be another person with a death sentence. She would have their name and address. But what could she do for them after she found them, other than watch them die?

Nothing. She couldn't help them at all.

Her hands shaking, Emily closed the folder and opened the browser. But when she logged into the Boards, the screen froze, and a message appeared. She knew it was from Xander even before she read it.

I'm sorry, but I can't stop the crawler. They'll know it was me, and they'll just find someone else. Come back, and we'll figure something out.

"Traitor." Emily closed the browser and was about to put the tablet away when another window popped open in the corner of the screen.

She had almost forgotten about Slayer and the news alert she had set up for him.

Apprehension gripped her. *What now?* She tapped the screen, and the news story filled her view.

The story wasn't about Slayer, though. It was about his father. The old Hollenbach was giving an interview.

Emily stared at Slayer's father. The old magnate beamed with health and charisma, as if his recent heart attack never happened. How did he manage to recover so quickly?

The young, golden-haired woman who was interviewing him seemed similarly puzzled. "You look fantastic, Mr. Hollenbach. What's your secret?"

The old Hollenbach laughed. "Thank you. I haven't felt this good in fifty years." Then he grew earnest, putting his hand over his heart. "I'll be honest with you. I didn't think I was going to make it. But I got lucky. I was given a second chance. Here's to two hundred more great years!"

Music started to play—a waltz. Hollenbach's face lit up, and he jumped from his chair. "May I have this dance?"

Without waiting for the woman's reply, he pulled her to her feet and lifted her into his arms. They waltzed around the room, the young journalist looking more out of breath than the old man who led her.

The interview ended, and another news story took its place. Something about the upcoming elections for the Chancellor of the Alliance.

But Emily was no longer paying attention. She put the tablet away, her mind reeling.

Two hundred years.

She guessed the meaning instantly.

Slayer's father had gotten an artificial heart. And not any heart—the same heart that killed Sylvia and the man in the strange suit. Titan SI 200. Made by Falcon and 3D Electronics.

And knowing how strict the old man had been when his own son had broken the law, Emily guessed something else.

Hollenbach didn't know about Falcon's plan. He didn't know about the missed lease payments and the termination dates that resulted in lethal heart failure. He would never have agreed to receive Falcon's heart if he'd known. Hollenbach experienced a real heart attack, after all. He would have to be a monster to wish it on others. And for all his strict rules, Emily didn't believe the old Hollenbach was cruel or unjust. It was his son who was the monster.

"Slayer!"

Suddenly it all fit together, and Emily was on her feet and pacing restlessly.

Of course! The old magnate wasn't out of danger at all. Far from it—the danger was closer than ever before and harder to escape.

His son got him an artificial heart—so he could turn it off and murder his father.

She had been merely annoyed by Slayer's nearly constant presence in the public spotlight ever since the last Race. Dinners, galas, interviews. Now the purpose of all these high-profile appearances was clear. Slayer—or rather Julian Hollenbach—was on a mission to get the wealthy elite of the megacity to love him. Why? Because he wanted to gain control of his father's company, BioPrintex.

But there would always be one more obstacle standing in his way. His father, who didn't think highly of him at all and could well choose to leave the company to someone more trustworthy and better qualified than his son.

Emily felt a chill. Was Hollenbach's first heart attack even an accident—or Slayer's handiwork as well, setting the stage for his planned and final crime? But that was done now. She could never prove it.

Then another thought made her shudder. Falcon and the old Hollenbach were no longer business partners, having severed all their ties and canceled all their joint ventures in a highly publicized fashion.

She had suspected from the start that Falcon had something to do with Hollenbach's heart failure. But Slayer had his own twisted motives to plot against his father.

What if Falcon and Slayer now joined forces?

Horrific as the thought was, it was like a fire stirred in

her core and rushed through her veins. Emily was no longer cold, no longer tired. She shook her head. "*No.*"

She would not let Slayer kill his father. She would warn the old magnate and gain an ally.

The thought of asking for his help had occurred to her before. Except now she had something to offer him in return—information that could save his life.

But for that, she had to find a loophole in the old man's security first.

She grabbed her tablet and got to work.

28
KAI

NO ONE SLEPT that night. When the morning came, they all stepped into the gray, chilly street and walked two blocks to where the hovercraft was already waiting.

Kai had never admired Leah more than in these last few minutes before she boarded the hovercraft that would transport her—and her alone—to Falcon's facility, where her failing heart would be removed and replaced with a new, artificial one.

Nobody was permitted to go with her—not even Val. Strict security rules. Take it or leave it.

Kai's silent fear for Leah was like smog around him, growing thicker as the time of her departure grew near, until he could hardly breathe.

Val was restless, his body in constant motion and his voice too loud. When he briefly fell silent, they could all hear him grinding his teeth.

Several times, Leah had to put a calming hand on her brother's arm. "I'll be fine," she told him patiently. "I'll be back in three days. You can manage without me until then, can't you?" she added with a smile. If she was afraid, she never showed it.

It took Kai back to his own arrival at the Training Center, and the cold panic that gripped him when Andy brought him straight to the surgery suite and handed him over to the doctor. Kai remembered the feeling all too well. The primal terror of metal tools cutting into flesh to take a part of him away, and the urgent desire to run, to escape, no matter what.

Then a medic stepped out of the hovercraft, an expectant look on her face. It was time to go.

Leah hugged her brother, then Ana, then everyone in the group, including the Rats. When it was Kai's turn, Leah's arms closed around him, light as air. Then she pulled back and smiled, "I need someone to water the tomatoes. Can I count on you *again?*"

"You got it," Kai said, his throat tight.

Leah nodded to him, then turned to the group. "Be good. Take care of each other. I'll see you in three days."

Val reached for her, and Leah squeezed her brother's hand one last time. Then the medic walked her up the steps into the cabin and strapped her down in her seat. The door slid shut behind them.

As soon as the hovercraft lifted into the air and sped off, Val turned away from it.

He glanced around him, making eye contact with a few people standing close to him before ordering, "All right. Let's go."

His gaze brushed Kai's face, a flash of something dark and almost hostile in his eyes. *Don't interfere*. Then the red-haired man stalked down the street, his shoulders tense and full of purpose. A smaller group detached from the larger one and followed their leader.

It took Kai a second to react. Val was heading away from the house. He caught Zip's arm as the man passed him. "Hey, where are you going?"

"Hunting," Zip said grimly, then yanked his arm free and walked on.

Max closed the rear. "We're going to catch the heart thief," he bragged, and jogged on to keep up with the long strides of his older and taller companions.

The thief from Falcon's video. That's who they were

after. Apparently, Val wasted no time.

Stunned, Kai watched the small group disappear around the corner. Part of him wanted to follow them and join in. But the other part wanted nothing to do with Falcon.

Besides, Val had never asked him to come, never even mentioned it to him. Was it because he sensed Kai's reluctance or for some other reason?

Later that day, after the search group returned to the house, Kai confronted Val. "How did the hunt go? Did you catch him?" It came out more like a taunt than a question.

Val narrowed his eyes. "Yeah. He was right there, waiting for us to find him. Same as your friend."

The mention of Emily stung. "So what, you work for Falcon now? If he tells you to hunt someone down and hand them over, you will?"

Val's face flushed almost the color of his hair. "I don't need him to tell me what's right and wrong, if that's what you mean. I can decide that for myself. But in this case, he and I are on the same side."

"You're sure about that?" Kai pressed. *What if he's lying to you?* he wanted to ask. *What if he's just using you to get what he wants?* But he thought of Leah and bit his tongue.

"I'm sure enough." Val glowered. "There's a psychopath on the loose, ripping out people's hearts, and someone has to stop him. So if you're not going to help, just stay out of my way." He pushed past Kai, slamming him with his shoulder.

The next day, Val and his group left right after breakfast. Ana, Zip, Karim, and Marco were there, their expressions grim and determined. So was Max, his chin high and spine stretched taut, as if to make himself taller.

Ana frowned at Kai, as if to say, *Why aren't you*

coming with us? You know we're doing it for Leah. But Val touched her shoulder, and she turned away.

The group headed out the door, and Kai turned and raced up the stairs to the greenhouse.

There was no one there. People had other things on their minds today, just as Leah had predicted.

She wanted him to water the tomatoes, so Kai watered the tomatoes. It took no time at all, so he watered all the other plants growing in the greenhouse as well, working methodically aisle by aisle, and taking care to do it right. When he was finished, he went through the list of other tasks that needed to be done in the greenhouse and settled on weeding.

If he was careful and kept his eyes on the weeding, he could almost pretend Leah was working next to him, instead of alone in Falcon's clinic, on the operating table, or perhaps already recovering after the surgery.

She'll be fine, he repeated to himself as he cut and pulled at the weeds. *She'll get a new heart and she'll be fine. The heart will be fine. There's nothing to worry about. She'll be back in three days, and the greenhouse will look great when she gets here.*

*

The night before Leah's return, Kai was still fighting with the weeds, determined to get the job done. Finally, exhausted from his work, he sat down next to a coiled water hose with his back against the wall and closed his eyes. He instantly fell asleep.

A voice woke him. Riko was bending over him, shaking his shoulder, her eyes bright and her voice urgent. "Kai! Get up! *She's back!*"

Kai blinked and rubbed his eyes, his muscles stiff and uncooperative. Then the meaning registered.

He sprang to his feet. Riko raced out the door, and he followed her downstairs, his heart hammering in his chest.

Animated voices reached him from the front room.

And there was Leah, with Val and Ana on either side, the rest of the group gathered around them. They must have just walked in.

Leah turned toward Kai, and relief washed over him.

She was all right! More than all right. She radiated health and strength. Gone was the pale complexion and the cautious manner of someone whose heart threatened to fail at any exertion. Leah's skin glowed with color and her movements were confident.

Kai moved closer, taking her in. There was no sign that she'd just undergone a major surgery. He'd used the high-tech healing serum when training for the Race, so he knew how powerful it was. Still, Leah's improvement was awe-inspiring, the stuff of magic and the supernatural more than science.

No wonder some people found biotechnology threatening.

"So what did I miss?" Leah looked around, her voice clear and strong like a bell. "What have you all been up to?"

Val and Ana exchanged a glance. "Not much," Ana said, too quickly. "Waiting for you, mostly."

A shadow passed across Leah's face, her eyes moving from Ana to her brother. But then she smiled again. "Well, no more waiting. Okay?"

Kai stepped closer, and the group parted to let him through. Leah's eyes lit up at the sight of him. But then she scanned him head to toe, frowning. "What happened to you? Is that... dirt?"

"What?" He looked down at his hands, his clothes. He was coated with dirt and never even noticed. He could only imagine what his face looked like.

"He hasn't left the greenhouse in two days," Riko offered.

Leah laughed. "Really? I want to see it."

Val caught her elbow. "Later. Okay? You need to rest."

Leah laughed again. "Val, I'm fine. Really." She gently pushed her brother's hand away, freeing herself. "And I *don't* need to rest anymore." She turned to Kai. "I want to see what Kai's been doing in the greenhouse."

Val's face creased with worry, and he threw Kai a dark look. But he didn't try to stop them.

Leah headed for the stairs. Kai and the rest of the group followed.

The celebration continued for the rest of the day. They all followed Leah around in a happy daze, reveling in her presence and marveling at her endless energy, unwilling to let her out of their sight. It was like a long, dark, toxic smog had lifted, and now the sun was out, and the air was fresh again.

But Kai found his gaze straying to Val and Ana. They conferred briefly, conspiratorially. Afterward, Val exchanged a few words with Zip, then with Marco, while Ana sought out Karim and Max.

By dinner time, Kai was certain. Val was planning another hunt. Tonight.

He was so focused on the hunters that he didn't notice Green at his elbow until he turned and nearly plowed through the boy. "Green. I didn't see you there. What's up?"

Green's eyes shone with intensity from behind his thick lenses. "I—I have to show you something." He spoke in a low voice, for Kai's ears only.

"What is it?" Kai couldn't tell from Green's expression if the news was good or bad.

"A new message on the Boards." Green's voice was

urgent but hollow, his eyes wide and staring as if he'd seen a ghost. "I think... it's from Syber." For some reason, his eyes flitted to Val, then quickly away.

Kai felt a stab of apprehension. If the message was from Syber, why wasn't Green happy? And why did he act like he didn't want Val to know? "Okay. Show me." He followed Green down the hall.

The message was a video clip, and both the scene and the person in it were instantly familiar. The narrow alley. The man in the insect suit. The same as in Falcon's video.

Except this footage was shot earlier. The man was still alive, stumbling down the alley. Running from someone.

Kai stared at the screen, his whole body tense in anticipation. In seconds, he would know if his suspicions were correct. He would see how the man in the insect suit really died.

As if in answer, the man stumbled, one knee buckling under him, and collapsed. A shudder ripped through his body and he clawed at his chest, ripping open his shirt. The camera zoomed in on a metal ID blinking on the man's chest. Then the ID went dark, and the man stilled.

He was dead.

Kai let out a sharp breath. *I knew it.*

The man was already dead when the thief found him. He died of heart failure. It was Falcon who killed him.

He glanced at Green, suddenly wondering how much he knew. But the eyes behind those thick lenses pointed back to the screen. "Keep watching. There's more."

A computer-generated text streamed across the frame. *3D Electronics is lying to you.*

"There's an audio, too." Green adjusted the volume, and an unfamiliar male voice urged in sync with the text. "Titan SI 200 kills people!" The voice became female.

"Spread the word, and fight back!"

But Kai's attention was on the figure in the dark, hooded coat that now leaned over the dead man. Familiar, slender fingers touched the man's chest. A strap of backpack came into view.

Shock slammed into Kai, and he exhaled sharply.

Images rushed through his mind. The same slender fingers holding a pencil, sketching quickly. The backpack—

Emily!

The video ended, but Kai's mind reeled, grasping at an explanation.

And then he had it.

Emily was fighting Falcon. She knew about his plan. That's why she always hated him.

And if so—

It was Emily who took the dead man's heart. It had to be.

"I think it's Syber, but I'm not sure. He hasn't signed the message," Green was saying. "Do you think I should tell Val?"

Val.

If Emily was the thief, then Val was hunting her down for Falcon.

Kai pushed to his feet, knocking the chair down behind him. "Is Val already gone?"

Green blinked. "Gone where?"

"Never mind. I have to go." Kai turned and rushed out of the room.

He could be wrong about everything.

But if he was right—he had to be there when Val found Emily.

It was his only chance to save her.

29
EMILY

EMILY HAD SPENT a sleepless night learning everything she could about the old Hollenbach, from his public speeches to his daily routines, and researching the layout of the BioPrintex corporate building and the security system within it, looking for a way in.

Several times she was close to giving up, her eyes burning and her head heavy. But she had to talk to Slayer's father. With his help, she could still turn it all around, and time was running out.

It was nearly dawn when her research finally paid off. She had found a possible way in.

Despite his company's focus on cutting-edge technology, the head of BioPrintex was rather old-fashioned. Unless special circumstances prevented it, he also favored entering his office building through the front entrance and the main lobby on the ground level. From there, he took a private elevator, used by no one but himself, to his executive office at the top of the building.

The elevator stopped at no other floors in between, although it did descend to the unused underground parking garage. The elevator was an antique, part of the original building design, dating back over two hundred years, kept in flawless working condition but lacking any modern security features. If Emily could get inside it before Hollenbach arrived in the morning, she would have almost a minute to talk to him.

It was a long shot. But there was no other way. And it was worth the risk.

Minutes later, she was running down one city block after another, her hood low and a mask covering her face. For once she was grateful for the smog drifting through the megacity. With the smog as her cover, her plan might actually succeed.

A block away from her destination, she slowed to a walk, then turned into an alley running alongside the BioPrintex building. A row of loading decks lined the wall, long unused judging by the thick layer of city dust coating the metal doors and the ID scanners next to them.

Emily wiped the first scanner with her sleeve. What if it was dead? She had no tools to pry open the door. But a faint red light told her the scanner was still online.

She angled the backpack close to the scanner. The light changed to green, and the door lock clicked open.

She sighed in relief. Kai's jacket worked as a universal entry key, but she worried it might not work against BioPrintex's security system.

She slipped inside and pulled the door closed behind her. The lock clicked shut.

She found a back staircase that took her to the underground garage. The garage was never used anymore, its lower levels wrapped in complete darkness. But here, on the top executive level, a faint light glowed on one wall. This was where Hollenbach's elevator stood at night, waiting for its only passenger to call it to ground level.

Emily walked toward the elevator. The faint glow came from the ID scanner by the door. She reached it and angled her backpack toward it. The door slid open, revealing a spacious cabin.

Emily hesitated. She had no idea if Slayer's father

would even let her speak, never mind listen to what she had to say. Why would he? He was one of the most powerful men in the megacity, and she was just a trespasser.

She had a bad feeling about the whole thing. But it was too late to turn back. She had to try.

Steeling herself, Emily stepped into the elevator, and the door slid shut behind her.

She moved to the corner and sat down on the floor, her back against the wall. She drew her knees close to her chest and waited.

She jerked awake when the elevator moved. She froze, not daring to move a muscle, cursing herself for falling asleep.

A moment later, the elevator stopped. The door slid open, and a man entered.

From the corner of her eye, she glimpsed leather shoes and tailored pants. The old Hollenbach.

The elevator doors slid shut, and the cabin slowly continued upward.

Emily looked up at the man. He towered over her, his tall, broad body perfectly still and his proud gaze fixed straight ahead.

She opened her mouth to address him, but the man spoke first, his deep voice ringing with annoyance. "Who are you, and how did you get in here?"

Gathering her courage, Emily pulled up to her feet. "It doesn't matter," she said to his profile. He still hadn't turned to look at her, as if he couldn't be bothered to redirect his gaze to something as trivial as a trespasser in his elevator. "I have to talk to you. It's about your son."

An angry grimace distorted Hollenbach's features, and he turned toward her. "What did he do now?" He scanned her from head to toe, as if looking for signs of damage that his son had inflicted.

Emily faltered. *Stick to the script.* She had rehearsed this. "It's not about what he did. It's about what he's *planning* to do."

Hollenbach's expression turned to scorn. "You should know that I do not respond to blackmail or to threats. If you're hoping for monetary gain, you will be disappointed."

"I don't want your money." Emily's blood ran hot. "I'm here to *warn* you. Your life is in danger!"

Shock registered on the old magnate's face. But only for a moment. The expression that replaced it was of cold dismissal. "I've heard enough of this nonsense," he ordered with finality.

Emily glanced at the display above the door, which marked their upward progress toward the man's office. They were almost there. "Please! Give me five minutes to explain!"

But the elevator door was already sliding open, and Hollenbach was stepping into his office, his silence her only reply.

Still Emily followed him, unwilling to give up. "No, please! You have to believe me. It's about your new heart. It—"

The words froze on her lips.

Standing in front of them was Slayer, his expression quickly turning from surprise to malicious enjoyment. "Father, I see you brought a guest."

"Get her out of here." The old magnate ordered with distaste.

Slayer didn't move. "But Father, she went to a lot of trouble to get here." He spoke with a fake, exaggerated deference. "Aren't you curious what she has to say?"

The old man spun to his son, his eyes flashing angrily and his composure coming undone. "What is this?" he hissed. "Did you put her up to it? Is this how you waste your time now?" Then he straightened. "Never mind. I don't have time for this. Unlike you, I take my duties to the company seriously."

Slayer's eyes narrowed. He slipped one hand into his pocket and took a step toward his father. It was as if Emily wasn't there anymore. "Maybe if you trusted me with something that matters, I would take *my* duties seriously too. But you treat me like a goddamn employee." He kept walking, his eyes burning into his father's face. "And I am *sick* of it—sick of *you,* old man."

Hollenbach's face twisted with outraged disbelief. "How dare you speak to me like that?" He glared at his son. "You've never accomplished anything in your life. I should have thrown you out and let you live in the gutters where you belong. You're a disgrace to this family, but I will *never* let you destroy my legacy."

Slayer closed the distance between him and his father in one fast leap, his hand flying out of his pocket.

"No!" Emily cried, expecting a gun.

But Slayer only pressed a hand to his father's chest. "You can go to hell." And he stepped away.

For a second, Hollenbach only stared at his son with disdain.

Then he shuddered and clutched his chest, his fingers clawing in agony at his suit, his shirt, then his flesh. His mouth opened as if to scream, but only a hollow moan of pain issued from it.

Then he fell to the floor and was still.

For a moment, Emily was too stunned to react. Then she rushed to the old man's side and checked his pulse. He had none. His heart had stopped beating.

She stared at the dead man, and the room swayed around her, memories rushing in. Sylvia collapsing in the gallery. Victor dead on the ground.

She had suspected it would happen, but now that it actually did, it didn't seem real.

She ripped the old man's shirt open and found the metal insert. It was dark.

Hollenbach was dead.

"I should thank you," Slayer's voice reached her, as if from far away.

"What?" Still on her knees, Emily turned, the floor and the walls settling down around her.

The look on Slayer's face chilled her to the core. Not a trace of remorse. Only... *triumph.* "I was going to wait a little longer. But you forced my hand. And I'm glad you did."

"You... killed him," Emily breathed. "You... killed your father."

"Yes. And you must be curious how I did it." Slayer lifted his hand. He wore a strange, metallic glove. "A remarkable piece of technology. It can suck all power from the heart with a single touch—or charge it to capacity." He pointed to a small toggle on the inside of the wrist. "You choose with a simple switch."

Emily stared at the metallic glove. Then the meaning of his words registered. "Then you can still save him! You can power the heart back up."

Slayer scowled. "And why would I want to do that?"

Emily got to her feet. "Because I saw what you did! You murdered him in cold blood. And you won't get away with it!"

"*I* murdered him in cold blood? *I* won't get away it?" Something dark and cruel gleamed in Slayer's eyes. "Why do you think *you*'re here?"

Dread shot through Emily, and she took a step back. *No.* Slayer couldn't do that. He couldn't pin his father's murder on her. Could he? She surveyed the walls, counting several security cameras. But she instantly knew it wouldn't be enough. The video could be altered, and she had no other witnesses.

It was a trap, and she had walked right into it.

"No one will believe you." She glanced toward the elevator. She was already silently calculating the distance and speed needed to reach it. It was her only way out.

Slayer took a step in her direction. "You're not thinking of making a run for it, are you?"

Desperation rose in her, and she scanned the room for a weapon. A heavy paper weight lay on the desk to her right. She leapt toward it, grabbing the bulky object and hurling it at Slayer. Then she sprinted for the elevator without waiting for her missile to hit the target.

She was already reaching for the call button when a powerful hand grabbed her shoulder and spun her around.

She caught a glimpse of Slayer's vicious grin. He was unharmed. She had missed.

"I can't let you leave yet."

Then the side of her head exploded with pain, and everything went black.

30
EMILY

A NOISE YANKED Emily back to awareness. Her eyes flew open, and she bolted upright to find a cracked cement ceiling and a blank wall, both unfamiliar.

She groaned. She was dizzy and nauseous, and the side of her head hurt. She touched it gingerly, just above the ear, and her fingers came away stained with blood.

Slayer. Her body tensed.

He had hit her on the head, and she had blacked out.

Fear gripped her, and she hurriedly scanned her body for more injuries. What else had he done to her? But except for some bruises and scrapes, she was fine. She was still wearing her long coat, and when she moved her hand, her fingers brushed the rough fabric of her backpack.

"Now for breaking news—"

A voice startled her, and she spun around, finding a tall window and a huge holographic screen outside it.

"Here is more on the shocking death of Marcus Hollenbach, the founder and CEO of BioPrintex," a male news anchor reported grimly. Smog slowly drifted past the screen, swallowing the last daylight and blurring a sea of skyscrapers beyond it.

Emily's skin prickled with anxiety as her mind struggled to recreate the events of the day leading up to this moment.

The old Hollenbach was dead...

She had tried to warn him but failed...

Was she a prisoner now? She quickly scanned the room around her. But an open door led to a hallway, and no one appeared to be watching her.

"The body of Marcus Hollenbach was found in his office earlier today by his son, Julian Hollenbach, now acting CEO of BioPrintex," the news anchor continued, while an inset image showed Hollenbach lying dead on the floor of his office.

Found? Emily glared at the screen. Slayer *murdered* him! And he could have killed her too.

But he *didn't* kill her.

The thought gave her pause, cutting right through the throbbing pain in her head.

Slayer hated her. She saw him kill his father in cold blood. He could have easily killed her, and disposed of the body, and nobody would ever suspect him.

And still, he didn't kill her—he let her go.

Why?

He wanted to frame her for his father's murder. That was the only explanation. But wouldn't it be easier to do if she wasn't alive to contradict him? She knew she was missing something...

On the screen, the anchor's report went on. "This death is made more tragic by the fact that, only weeks ago, Hollenbach had narrowly avoided death from heart failure, and had subsequently made an impressive recovery thanks to"—here the anchor's voice brightened noticeably—"a new, cutting-edge artificial heart produced by 3D Electronics—Titan SI 200."

Emily shivered, her mind clearing.

The heart!

She grabbed her backpack and dug inside it. Victor's heart had been inside it when she walked into Hollenbach's elevator. Had Slayer taken it from her?

But no. Her fingers closed around it, and she lifted it halfway to see it, before putting it back.

Victor's heart was still there, and so was Kai's jacket and her tablet. Slayer had taken neither.

On the screen, the anchor's voice turned solemn, "Citizens of the Alliance, the lead investigator has just issued a statement. Hollenbach's death was *not* due to any flaw in his artificial heart. It was *murder.*" The anchor paused for effect. "And we now know the killer's name—*Emily Starr.*"

Emily gasped as her own image filled the screen. In it, she knelt next to Hollenbach's body, her hands digging into his bare chest and her eyes glaring.

More images of her flashed on the screen, from close-ups to full-body views of her standing, walking, or running in her long coat, with her hood deep over her eyes and a mask covering the rest of her face.

Above the images, a blood red banner screamed on repeat, *Wanted for murder. Reward for capture dead or alive. Wanted for murder. Reward for capture dead or alive.*

"But there's more." On the screen, the anchor paused for effect, and an image of a man's ripped, gaping chest filled half of the screen. "Starr is now suspected of at least one other murder targeting another artificial heart recipient, in which the device was brutally removed from the body. Authorities are saying she may be acting on behalf of a radical anti-biotechnology group known as the Collectors."

"What?" Emily pulled herself to her feet and leaned against the wall, fighting the vertigo.

She hated the Collectors. But so did a lot of people, including a vast majority of the sector dwellers. The murder of Hollenbach was one thing. They would hunt her for the bounty. But if they actually believed she worked for the Collectors—that she killed in their name—she would never make it out of the city alive.

Slayer wanted her dead after all.

Emily gritted her teeth.

Now she knew why he had brought her up here. He wanted her to see the news. He wanted her paralyzed with fear.

Like on cue, Slayer appeared on the screen, looking stricken as he gave a statement to a reporter.

Emily glared at him. "You want to kill me? You'll have to catch me first."

She would have to hide for a while. But her fight wasn't over. She still had her tablet. She still had Falcon's database. She'd figure something out.

Bending down, she grabbed her coat off the floor and shrugged it on. She was about to pick up her backpack when her hand brushed against a hard object in the deep pocket of her coat.

She froze. Then reached into the pocket and brought the object out.

Slayer's glove!

Emily stared at it.

She could ditch the glove right now, get rid of the evidence.

Except... Slayer was too cunning to make it that easy. There had to be more to his plan.

And then the full meaning sunk in, and she let out a shuddering breath.

The glove didn't just suck the power out of the heart. It could also do the opposite—it could power a dead heart back on. "*Charge it to capacity,*" were Slayer's words.

Which meant that Emily couldn't get rid of the glove, and she couldn't hide.

She finally had a defense against Falcon—and she couldn't give it up now. She would find each person with the artificial heart, starting with those whose lease was late, and she would recharge it for them. And she would do it over and over again, as many times as it took. She would save them all.

Her heart pounding with resolve, she slipped the glove back into her pocket and shrugged on the backpack. She turned toward the door, ready to leave, when her eyes strayed to the window.

A fashion update was now playing on the screen. Apparently, the current hot trend was shoes that resembled robotic prostheses and shirts with one arm styled to look artificial as well, in honor of the upcoming No Limits Race.

But above the fashion story, a streaming red banner continued to scroll, *Wanted for murder. Reward for capture dead or alive. Wanted for murder. Reward for capture dead or alive,* along with her picture.

Emily's heart sunk.

She would never make it. How could she save anyone before she got caught? And then, even if she didn't get killed, she could do nothing in prison. The database and now the glove would be useless if no one else knew what they meant and what they could do, if no one else carried on her fight.

If she got caught, Falcon would win, and it would all be for nothing. Everything she'd been through. Everything *Kai* had been through.

No. Falcon won't win. I won't let that happen.

People had to know what was going on. She had to warn them, as many of them as possible. She had to share what she knew before it was too late.

But how? Where could she find the right people, people who would listen to her, before the wrong ones found her?

And then she knew—she could picture the place and the safest route to get there.

There was no time to waste. With every moment she

delayed, more people would be out there in the streets, hunting for her.

She raised her hood and rushed out the door.

31
KAI

KAI CLIMBED the last flight of stairs to the top floor and faced the long hallway ending with a narrow window. A thick layer of dust covered the floor, untouched by human foot. No one had entered or left any of these apartments for a very long time, ruling them out as Emily's hiding place. But he would check each one, anyway.

Val's instructions had been clear. Besides, Kai wanted to know for himself.

Fifteen minutes later, all the apartments proved empty, the door unlocked to reveal floors and furniture coated with more dust. The only trace of human presence were the footprints left by Kai's own prosthetic feet.

He paused by the window at the end of the hallway and looked out. A forest of cement apartment buildings stretched before him, all of them abandoned and some beginning to crumble. All that was missing was a web of heavy ropes controlled by grinding motors, and it could have been the course he remembered from the Race. The one that almost cost Dynamo his life.

For a moment, the floor underneath Kai's feet transformed into a rope, the walls vanishing around him. And then the rope fell away, and Kai was falling...

He leaned against the wall, his pulse racing, before turning and heading back to the staircase.

He ran down the stairs, floor after floor after floor, down to the ground level. There, he pushed out the door. The landscape was all gray cement and dust under a darkening sky. Dusk was falling.

Ana and Karim sat on the outside steps two staircases down. Kai crossed in their direction.

"Find anything?" Ana asked him.

Kai shook his head. "Nothing. You?"

"No," Ana admitted coldly.

Karim glanced at the buildings around them. "This was the last one, right?" He straightened and groaned as his spine cracked. "I don't know about you, guys. But I'm ready to head back."

Zip and Marco were already walking their way, back from their search of two other buildings. Max was right behind them.

"Anything?" Ana asked.

They all shook their heads. Marco leaned against the wall. Max plopped down on the ground, then lay flat on his back, closing his eyes. "I need a nap."

They had been out here all day and must have climbed up and down thousands of steps. They were all exhausted. Even Kai's legs were sore, as if his prostheses were suddenly ten times heavier.

Val emerged from the building on the left, heading toward them. He was limping badly, but his expression was still determined.

Zip poked Max with his shoe. "Get up. Unless you want to stay here."

"Yeah, Max." Marco pitched in. "You should stay. You can have a hundred apartments, with a hundred different beds. You can be king here."

Max scrambled to his feet. "By myself? So the heart thief can get me? No way!"

Ana rolled her eyes. "He doesn't want *your* heart. I

already told you."

But Max still looked skeptical.

Val scanned their faces and frowned. He didn't even have to ask. "Don't worry. We'll find him. We'll come back to search the next block tomorrow. But that's it for today. Come on." He turned and led the way home.

*

They heard the voice coming from the living room as soon as they entered the house. "...As the investigation into this new and shocking murder continues, a city-wide search for the killer is already under way."

Blood drained from Val's face, and he rushed down the hallway. Kai and the others followed.

"Leah?" Val stalked into the room, where the whole group had gathered in front of the TV to watch the news.

Leah hurried to her brother. "I'm right here. Are you alright?"

Val quickly scanned her body and sighed with relief. "I'm fine. I was worried about you."

But Leah only pulled him toward the TV. "You have to watch this. Two people were killed."

Kai stared at the screen, his gut twisting with a terrible premonition.

"Prior to their tragic death," the news anchor went on, "both victims had suffered life-threatening cardiac failure and were implanted with Titan SI 200, a new state-of-the-art replacement heart."

Two images filled the screen. In one, Marcus Hollenbach lay dead on the floor of his office. In the other, harder to look at, Victor Harding lay in a pool of blood, his chest torn and a gaping hole where his heart used to be.

Kai stared from one image to another, trying to make

sense of what he was seeing.

"Come on, you don't need to see this." Val tried to take Leah's arm, as if to escort her out.

But she moved away. "Yes, I do! I need to know what's going on. You can't protect me forever."

"While we may never know the true motives behind the murders," the anchor went on, "the killer is believed to have acted on behalf of the radical anti-biotechnology group known as the Collectors."

Kai hung on every word, trying to grasp the connections, bracing himself for what was still to come.

He caught dark looks exchanged around the room. The Collectors were universally hated.

"A private police force is now sweeping the city to bring this dangerous criminal to justice," the anchor continued. "But all citizens are asked to be vigilant, and a substantial reward will be paid for any information leading to her arrest."

"*Her?*" Val spun around wildly. "It's a woman?"

The two images changed on the screen. Now a figure in a dark coat knelt next to each victim. In the image of Harding, only her hands were visible, resting on the man's still intact chest. But in the image of Hollenbach, she was facing the camera.

"The killer has been identified as Emily Starr," the anchor announced in a somber tone, "and she is wanted dead or alive on charges of first-degree murder."

It was like Kai's chest had been ripped open and *his* heart yanked out.

Emily's life was in danger.

"*No*," he said fiercely, his hands curling into fists. Whatever it all meant, whatever Emily did, he still believed in her. She wasn't a murderer. When did the news ever tell the whole truth? For all he knew, it could *all* be lies.

He was already turning, when someone slammed into him, and he hit the wall.

Val gripped the front of his shirt. "Where *is* she?"

Leah was next to them in a flash, pulling at her brother's hands. "Val! What are you doing? Stop it!"

"He knows her!" Val growled. "He can lead us to her!" But he let go of Kai's shirt.

The group had formed a tight circle around them.

Leah turned to Kai. "Is that true? Who is she?"

"She was my Agent in the Race and my... best friend," Kai said. "But she *didn't* do it," he said with conviction.

"How do you know?" Ana studied him shrewdly. "Do you have any idea what she's been up to?" She scowled at him. "Your *best friend* cut you loose, didn't she?"

Anger stirred in Kai's chest, hot and reckless, but he pushed it down. He couldn't afford to pick a fight right now. He had to stay calm and make them understand.

"Yeah, she cut me loose." Each word choked him like a stone in his throat. "But even so—I *know* her." He looked from one person to another, desperate to convince them. "I *know* her, and I *trust* her. And I'm telling you—she *didn't* do it."

Val shook his head, his eyes burning into Kai's. "Not good enough—"

Just then, Axer burst into the room. "You guys!" he panted. "I *saw* her! I saw the killer!"

"Where have *you* been?" Leah frowned.

But Val grabbed the boy and spun him toward him. "*Where?*"

"Near Ronny's factory."

The cage race.

Before any of them could stop him, Kai pushed past them and sprinted out of the room, out of the house, and into the street.

32
KAI

NIGHT WAS ALREADY FALLING on the city as Kai raced to the factory.

By now, the news of the wanted murderer and the bounty on her head was all over the sector. Every few blocks, a group of grim-faced men and women stared up at a holographic screen cast by a drone. They turned after Kai as he passed, their eyes narrowed with suspicion and greed. A few even tried to follow but quickly fell behind.

Kai clenched his jaw and ran harder.

He rounded a corner. The factory was only a block away now. A violent roar of the crowd came from the building, the drum of their fists and boots pounding on metal like a frantic heartbeat, echoing down the dark street. No cage race produced such frenzy. It had to be something more.

Emily.

Kai sprinted for the door and rushed inside.

Up close, the crowd's roar became a chant. "Kill the monster! Kill the monster!"

Terror slashed through Kai. What if he was too late? He spun around.

The main floor of the factory was crammed with people, all pushing and yelling to get closer to the race track. The observation deck was packed as well, the crowd stomping and beating their fists against the wire cage. More people perched on top of the machines or hung from the wire barrier. All eyes were fixed on the track, glaring, and the same chant rose from every throat.

"Kill the monster! Kill the monster! Kill the monster!"

Kai swiftly climbed a metal railing near the door, desperate to see.

And there she was—standing alone in the center of the opening where the race track began and ended. She held a long steel pole in one hand. But she wasn't wielding it like a weapon. At least not yet. She was trying to talk to the crowd over the noise!

Relief surged through him. He had found her. He could help her.

Just then, a man hanging from the wire wall swung his arm wildly—and Emily recoiled, a grimace of pain on her face as a rock hit her shoulder.

"Emily!" Kai called out hoarsely.

But only a few people nearby turned his way, tossing him dark looks. Emily couldn't hear him. He had to get inside the cage.

He started pushing through the crowd, trying to elbow his way forward. "Let me through! Let me through!" But the crowd was packed tight like a wall. He couldn't get to her.

"Kill the monster! Kill the monster!" The chant went on, gaining intensity.

Kai glanced around him in desperation.

Ronny stood off to the side, waving his arms and yelling into a microphone that clearly wasn't working.

Kai tore through the crowd in his direction. "You have to stop this! They're going to kill her!"

Ronny was frantic and red-faced from screaming. "Oh yeah? Well, it's her choice. I offered to hide her when she marched in here." Disappointment soured Ronny's features. "Now they're going to trash the place!"

Kai glared at the man in disgust. "*Hide* her, huh? So you can collect the bounty?"

"What about you, Sand Runner? You think with those fancy legs of yours, you can snatch her first?" Ronny narrowed his eyes. "Last time I saw you, you sounded pretty desperate for cash."

"If anybody touches her—"

The chant of the audience turned into a wild roar. "*Yeahhh!* Get her! Make her pay!"

"Emily!" Kai spun away from Ronny—and his gaze met Val's. He stood near the door with Ana, Zip, and the others right behind him.

Something dark and menacing flashed in Val's eyes, and he started in Kai's direction.

Kai didn't wait for the group to reach him. He raced past Ronny toward the nearest wall and started climbing the massive, industrial shelving that once stored sheets of metal and bales of wire. He quickly got to the top of the shelving, at least twenty feet high, and ran across the top of it toward the cage.

Overhead, at regular intervals, long steel beams stretched from one wall to another, supporting complex light fixtures. Kai raced under the first beam, then under the second, but he leapt high for the third one, grabbing it with both hands. He swiftly climbed on top of it and stood up.

He was a good forty feet above the ground now, with the beam no wider than four inches and only sharp-edged machines to break his fall. But the beam passed right over the cage. It would lead him straight to Emily.

Kai took a deep breath and started running.

"Look! Look! Up there!" People shouted from the deck, hands pointing. The stomping and rattling of the cage continued, but the chant had died down. For the moment, the crowd's attention was on him.

"Listen to me! I came to warn you!" Emily's voice rose above the noise, and Kai stumbled, a stab of pain in his chest, as if someone stuck a knife there.

Part of him had lost hope that he'd ever hear her voice again.

"Emily!" he called to her before jumping off the beam.

She looked up, watching him with wide eyes as he landed in front her. "Kai?" Then she shook her head. "You shouldn't be here." There was a large bruise on her cheek and a cut over her eyebrow.

Kai hurried toward her, reaching for her hand. "Yes, I should." He wanted to pull her close and never let go. But now wasn't the time. "I know you didn't do it. And we're still a team."

Emily studied him, emotions flickering across her face. Then she pulled her hand away. "This has nothing to do with you, Kai. You have to go right now. *Please.*"

Kai straightened, holding her gaze. "I'm not going anywhere without you."

"A damn killer!" A woman shouted from the deck, and a rock sailed from her fingers. Kai leapt forward, shielding Emily's body with his. The rock hit him in the arm. Hard.

"Kai, don't!" Emily said. Then she shouted to the woman, "I'm *not* a killer! It's all lies! But I can tell you who the killer is, if you just let me speak!"

The stomping and rattling of the wire barrier grew louder as the crowd vented its displeasure.

"Hey, you!" A bearded man yelled to Kai. "Sand Runner! You got your ass kicked here the last two times." The man held up another rock. "How about you get the hell out of the way and let us deal with her!"

Kai glared at the man. "How about you shut up and listen to what she has to say?"

The rock shot through the air in his direction but Kai was faster, leaping out of the way. He glanced down at the rocks that already littered the ground and started stomping on them, stone crushing to dust under his prosthetic feet.

"She needs to shut up! Killers don't get to talk!" A man shouted angrily.

A woman next to him added, "Nobody cares what she has to say!"

"I do," a voice boomed behind Kai, and he turned.

Death Wish had walked into the cage. He nodded to Kai, then raised his hand to the audience, signaling for them to quiet down. The crowd shifted, heads turning in surprise. But the uproar ceased.

"Sand Runner saved my life." Death Wish's voice echoed in the sudden silence. "You all saw it. He had the victory in his hand. But he made a choice. He risked his life to save mine. So I'm asking you now to show him that you respect that choice, and let this woman speak."

Kai caught Emily's eye, and the exhilaration he remembered from the Race surged through him. His veins thrummed with the sudden certainty that he could do anything, climb any height, break any speed—for her—because she believed in him.

"But she's a monster!" A white-haired man's voice shattered the silence. "She killed them all! It was on the news!"

Kai stepped forward, already opening his mouth to speak. But Emily put her hand on his arm. Then she turned to the white-haired man.

"I didn't kill *any* of them." She spoke as loudly as she could without shouting. "I tried to help them. I tried to warn them." Her breathing was rapid, but she kept her voice firm. "And since when do you believe everything you see on the news?"

Now the questions came from all sides. "If you didn't kill them, then who did?" a woman demanded.

"3D Electronics did. Falcon did," Emily said. "Not

me."

The crowd murmured darkly. "That's what the message on the Boards said too," a voice shouted.

"That's right," Emily went on. "And you know why he killed them? Because they couldn't pay the lease they owed him—the lease on their own heart! So he turned them off and killed them. I saw two people die like that." Emily glanced at Kai, pain and anger contorting her face.

So the rumor Green had told him was true.

The crowd shifted around them, voices rising as people reacted to the grim revelation.

"What?"

"They were *leasing* their hearts?"

"How is this allowed?"

"What about Hollenbach?" someone protested. "He was too poor to pay his lease too?"

Emily hesitated. "No. His son killed him. I was trying to warn him, but I was too late."

No one challenged that. The questions were drying out, the crowd's agitation and hostility seeping away. Emily glanced at Kai with hope.

Then a voice made them both turn. "Too late to rip out his heart, you mean?"

Val stood at the cage's entrance, his eyes burning into Emily.

33
KAI

"YOU JUST MADE some pretty big accusations," Val went on, his voice cold and skeptical and his eyes still fixed on Emily's face. "But the news didn't lie about everything. You *did* rip out a man's heart, didn't you?"

Dead silence followed Val's question, all murmurs ceasing as the crowd waited.

Emily took a step back, color draining from her cheeks. The steel pole she was holding slipped from her hand and hit the ground.

Kai turned to Val. "What are you doing?"

Val ignored him. But someone else stepped into the cage behind him.

Leah.

Ana, Zip, Karim, Marco, and Max stood at the edge of the cage, having pushed their way to the front of the crowd.

Kai tried to catch Leah's eye, but her gaze stayed on Emily.

"Emily Starr, answer the question," someone yelled down from the deck. "We want to know if you took the heart."

Emily swallowed. "Yes," she finally said. "Yes, I took it. From Victor Harding, after he was already dead." She slowly took off her backpack and reached inside it. With shaking fingers, she pulled out the artificial heart and held it up.

Agitated murmurs rose around them again, the crowd staring at the device in Emily's hand.

"May I?" Leah had moved closer, her eyes bright. "I have one just like it." She indicated her own chest, smiling. "But I never got to see it."

"Leah." Val started in his sister's direction, but she stopped him with a glance.

Emily handed her the heart, and Leah turned it in her hands, examining it. Then she looked up at Emily. "Why did you take it?"

Emily glanced to her side, her gaze meeting Kai's for a moment, as if the answer was for him. Then she turned back to Leah. "Because I wanted to figure out how it works—how Falcon can turn it off. So I can stop him the next time he tries to kill someone."

"And did you figure it out?" Val cut in sharply.

Emily hesitated, her hand moving into the pocket of her coat. "I—"

"Well, did you figure it out or not?" Val pressed.

Kai picked up the steel pole from the ground, his eyes on Val. "Take it easy."

Emily let her hand slip out of her pocket, still empty. "Not yet."

"Then you know what I think? I think you're lying!" Val shouted angrily. "You said Falcon can stop the hearts. But I don't believe you. The heart can beat for two hundred years. Two hundred years!"

"Val." Leah put a calming hand on her brother's arm. Then she turned to Emily. "I believe you," she said in a strong voice that carried to the farthest row of the audience. "And I hope you figure it out, like you said." She handed back the heart, her expression serious now.

Emily took it and replaced it in her backpack. "I will."

Val shook off Leah's hand and stalked away to the edge of the cage. Ana instantly moved to his side, and the two of them exchanged a glance.

Kai made himself look away, but adrenaline surged through him. Val was planning something. Would he still try to make good on his promise to Falcon and deliver the heart thief? Kai didn't want to believe it, but he couldn't risk being wrong.

He gripped the steel pole tighter and leaned toward Emily. "We need to go," he said under his breath.

"You're right. You do," Leah cut in, also in a whisper. "But it shouldn't be back with us." Pain crossed her face. "My brother... is out of his mind. You're not safe."

Kai gave a slight nod, feeling Val's stare on his back. "I understand. Thank you. For everything."

Leah let her fingers brush against his hand. "Be careful—and good luck." Then she nodded to Emily and walked away.

The crowd stirred again. "So what—we just let her walk out of here?" someone yelled.

Emily lowered her head. "Kai, I don't want you here," she said sharply. "You need to go right now."

Kai took her hand in his. "Not a chance."

Emily's tone softened. "Please. Look around. Does it look like I'm going anywhere?"

A distant crack and hiss of machines came from the far part of the track, then got louder and closer.

Death Wish walked up to Kai. "What are you waiting for, Sand Runner?" He spoke in a low voice. "You'll miss your race." He nodded to Emily. Then, with startling speed, he leapt to the gate of the cage and pulled it shut, locking everyone out.

Kai tightened his grip on Emily's fingers. "Come on!" And they took off running down the track, past grippers, paint nozzles, and stamping presses that were coming to life around them.

The crowd was hushed in surprise for a moment. Then a frenzy of shouting voices, stomping boots, and rattling metal broke out.

But Kai and Emily were already at the other end. "Now what?" Emily asked.

The track looped back along the other wall of the building.

"Over here!" someone said, and Emily's head snapped in that direction. "Xander?"

A young man poked his head from behind a loose board in the wall, beckoning them closer. "Quick!"

Emily hesitated, then climbed over. Kai followed. As soon as he was in, the board swung in place behind them. They were in an office.

Kai watched the stranger tensely. Who was he? And how did he know they were here? Emily had never mentioned him.

Xander crossed the room and pulled open a door leading to a basement. "This way. It connects to a tunnel. It'll take us out of the city."

Emily planted her feet in place and crossed her arms. "You're spying on me?"

"I'm just making sure you're alright." Xander turned his strange gaze on Kai—one eye dark, the other light. "This place is dangerous. Horrific accidents happen all the time."

The meaning clicked, and Kai said, "It was you who posted the message."

Xander inclined his head.

Emily frowned. "What message? What are you talking about?"

"I almost died in a race here," Kai explained. "It was... pretty bad. But someone posted a message to alert Neen and she came to get me. She fixed my legs."

Emily shuddered, her hand finding Kai's again. "Fixed your legs?" Then she stared Xander in the eye, not even masking her distrust. "Why are you helping *us?*"

The emphasis was hard to miss.

Suspicion and jealousy stirred in Kai, one fueling the other. He could tell Emily and Xander had a history. But what was it? He didn't even know where *he* stood with her.

Xander smiled. "Like I said, just making sure you're alright. Both of you."

Emily gripped Kai's hand more tightly. Then she turned back to Xander. "Okay. We'll go with you. But it doesn't mean anything."

"Of course not," Xander's strange eyes glinted. "Now we better hurry."

He stepped aside to let her and Kai enter the basement. Then he followed, pulling the door closed behind them.

THE END

About the Author

Vera Brook is a neuroscientist turned science fiction and fantasy writer.

To learn more about Vera's writing and other creative endeavors, visit her website, and follow her on Twitter or Goodreads.

www.verabrook.com
@VeraBrook1

Made in the USA
Middletown, DE
18 September 2023

38662086R10139